Jane Eyre's Rival:
The Real Mrs Rochester

Jane Eyre's Rival: The Real Mrs Rochester

Published by Blue Ocean Publishing
St John's Innovation Centre
Cambridge CB4 0WS
United Kingdom

www.blueoceanpublishing.biz

A catalogue record for this book is available from the British Library.

ISBN 978-1-907527-00-5

First published in the United Kingdom in 2011 by Blue Ocean Publishing.

Jane Eyre's Rival:
The Real Mrs Rochester

Clair Holland

Blue Ocean Publishing

Jane Eyre's Rival: The Real Mrs Rochester

If I could have our time again, I would have talked less and kissed you more.

I am not the same person today as I was yesterday. Because of you, something inside me changed. Because of you, I rediscovered a part of myself I had buried so deeply that even I thought it lost forever. Because of you, I learned more about me. You made the writing of this book possible. You gave me my hero. And more than that; the memory of you and your passionate embrace gave me the strength to carry on and continue writing when words failed me.

This novel is more than just a book. It's up to you to decide what else it is. When did I write it? In the hours between sleeping and waking. In the time of dreams. In the time of possibilities when our imagination takes flight. In the time when the night becomes our reality and the morning is a lifetime away.

All our experiences change us, one way or another. What we choose to do with those experiences and how we choose to use them, is up to us.

Would I do it again? In a heartbeat.

Thank You

I want to thank those girlfriends who supported me throughout the writing of this book, who believed in the power of the story and who believed in my ability to capture it and write it down. They are, firstly, Lesley, whose goose bumps made me believe that I might have a story worth telling. Secondly, Sarah W, whose continued cajoling for the first chapter encouraged me actually to sit down and write it. Thirdly, my thanks to Sarah Frossell, who taught me everything I know that's worth knowing about the use of language. Fourthly, to my girlfriends who share my love of the countryside and all things equestrian and whose company, both on horseback and on the ground, has brightened my days. Next, my thanks to Louise. Our lives often seemed to be running along parallel tracks, and the support that we were able to give each other when we needed it most, and the discussions that we had around the dynamics of relationships that weave through this book helped me shape it in ways that that I hope will enrich your lives, my readers, as much as they have mine.

My thanks also to the Melton Mowbray Carnegie Museum of Hunting for advice on nineteenth century ladies' riding dress, and to the Shoe and Boot Museum in Northampton. I also found the two houses of Grimsthorpe Castle and Stoke Rochford Hall in South Lincolnshire fundamental in helping me to imagine the Thornfield Estate and gardens, the kind of life that The Real Mrs Rochester would have lived, and the things she would have seen from her windows. My special thanks to the delightful staff at Burghley House in Stamford whose detailed knowledge of the house and its history inspired my imagination to take flight in the servants' passageways and secret doorways of the Thornfield Hall of my mind.

Mr Colin Henderson also deserves a special mention. As a previous Head Coachman to our glorious Queen Elizabeth II, in service at the Royal Mews in London, he provided me with those supporting details that only a coachman who has spent a lifetime with carriages and carriage horses would know.

To all of my other girlfriends, too numerous to mention, who helped and supported me in ways that I possibly didn't even notice at the time, thank you. A word here, a turn of phrase there, a kindness; all of which appeared to come together seamlessly to be just what I needed at just the right time. My thanks too, although they will never know it, to Dudley and Spanner, my two cats, who snuggled up next to me as I sat and wrote this book while it was dark outside and until the sun came up.

Finally, and most importantly, with my last poet's breath on the page, I would like to whisper my thanks to the man who is my hero. You know who you are. Your kiss brought me back to life and allowed me to reconnect with those parts of myself I was afraid that I had switched off for good and possibly lost forever. Your embrace breathed life back into me when I thought that I would never find passion again. Because of you, I found the life and the energy I was searching for. Passion was within me all the time. But you gave it wings and with it set me free. Because of you I learned to fly again.

I shall be forever grateful.

A Letter to Caitlin: From a Mother to a Daughter

I have written this book for you to help you learn about relationships. It contains within its pages those things that it's important to know regarding the ways in which people communicate with each other and those things that I wish someone had told me on my journey through life to adulthood. I have written this book for you so that you can learn from my experiences whilst you reflect on the meaning of your own. I have written this book to ask you to remember to always look at things from another perspective and to remind you that everyone has a voice, even though what they say may be different from what you currently believe to be true.

I want this book to teach you that the dynamics of a relationship will change depending on the people within that relationship and that, just because you can't make a relationship work with one particular person, it doesn't mean that every relationship will be like that. I also want to remind you that people change. The person you are today is not the same person you were last year and is not the same person you will become. Who you will be, how you will behave and the way you will think about the world are all flexible depending on things like experience, motivation, beliefs, who you spend time with and the ways in which you are valued and supported by your friends.

Recognise that there isn't just one person out there for you who will love you for who you truly are. There are many of them. And all you have to do is to find just one.

So I give you this book with a wish on the wind and a prayer for your happiness. If you find yourself in a relationship that doesn't work for you, end it. Be brave. Have courage. Move on. Take the learning and let the rest go. Guilt, regret and fear don't help us. They make us frightened to try again in case we fall, hurting ourselves and others in the process.

I was afraid of motherhood. Afraid that I wouldn't be up to the task. Afraid of the responsibility. And afraid that you would need more from me and of me than I would be able to give. You taught me not to be afraid. And more than that. You taught me that if I got it wrong, as I often did, and still do at times, that in the kindness and generosity of your spirit, and because you love me as I love you, that you would forgive me so that I needn't be afraid.

So learn from me as I learned from you and face your fears, my love. Let them give you courage. I asked the Universe for a daughter and it gave me so much more.

Author's Prologue

As a teenager, *Jane Eyre* was one of my favourite novels. I was fascinated by the passion that could unite two people across time and space so that each hears the other's very soul cry out to them, whereupon they rush to each other's side to be physically reunited at last. As an impressionable teenager, I thought the book hopelessly romantic and resolved that one day I too would fall in love with, and marry, a brooding hero.

Thank God I didn't.

Ever since I can remember, I have always been intrigued by people and relationships. Over the years I noticed how differently I behaved with each new boyfriend; adapting my own sense of self to match their expectations, whilst desperately trying to retain a sense of my own identity. Of course, somewhat predictably in retrospect, the relationships didn't work out, and it was only when I knew myself well enough not to want to change, that I met the man whom I was subsequently to marry.

When I began dating I was always looking for 'The One'. For some reason, possibly because of romantic fiction of the likes of *Jane Eyre* and *Wuthering Heights*, I believed that there was only one person in the world with whom I could ever be truly happy. It was my mission in life as a woman to find that man and then to live happily ever after, surrounded by children and dogs and perhaps a few chickens.

I eventually learned, after much searching and not a little trial and error, that there are many people out there in the world with whom I could have led a happy and fulfilled life. I have written this book in the hope that, whilst reading it, you are able to learn some of the difficult things about relationships that it took me half a lifetime and a degree in psychology to finally understand.

For You, the Reader

The structure of this book is slightly unusual. You will find within its pages what is, effectively, two books and two stories. Entangled and intertwined over time and linked by the bonds of family, love and passion.

The timeline changes with each chapter, so if you find that you want to read the nineteenth century novel in its entirety, you will need to read chapter one and then the even numbered chapters of the book. You will find the more modern, psychological explorations of the themes in the book relating to love and relationships in the chapters in-between.

To help you to differentiate the chapters slightly more easily, I have used a traditional font for the historical novel and a more modern font for those chapters that explore the dynamics of relationships. You will also notice that within the modern chapters, I mention *Psychologies Magazine* a number of times. This is a real magazine, published in the UK. As both a woman and as a psychologist I can't recommend it highly enough in the sense of helping you to understand the most important relationship that you will ever have; the relationship that you have with yourself. Because it is only once you have a great relationship with yourself, that you can go on to have a great relationship with anyone else, be they your parents, siblings, friends, work colleagues or lovers.

One way or another, we are all work-in-progress. I hope that this book makes a positive contribution to your life's journey and to the quality of your relationships within it.

An Introduction to *Jane Eyre*

If you have read Charlotte Brontë's work, her novel, *Jane Eyre*, published in 1847, will need no introduction and no explanation.

If, however, you are not familiar with Jane Eyre and the journey of her life, you may want to read the synopsis of her story which you will find at the end of this book. She was, after all, the second Mrs Rochester so it seems a fitting place to position it.

I cannot claim that it will be the best précis of the *Jane Eyre* story that you will ever read. However, it will provide the background knowledge that you need and fill in any gaps, so that what I have written for you here in *Jane Eyre's Rival: The Real Mrs Rochester* makes sense to you and you understand the references that I make to *Jane Eyre* within my own parallel version of the story.

Chapter 1

You almost didn't realise it was raining until you noticed that the world outside the window was no longer silent. Despite the fragile evening sun sinking low and orange in the west, fat, heavy, corpulent droplets fell from a charcoal sky overhead to beat a rhythmic percussion on the uneven roofs and crooked chimneys of old Cambridge. The gargoyles' stony faces, fractured and split by the frosts and thaws of centuries, became grotesque fountains, spurting and spluttering liquid gold down into the courtyards and private gardens of one of the oldest universities in England.

Lisa looked up. In its final throes of passion, the sunset was ebbing away, slipping between the skyscape and the clouds. It was getting dark and the library was closing. Around her, students were collecting up their things and chatting to each other in hushed voices, so as not to provoke the reproach of the librarians. She dismissed her thoughts, closed down the computer and collected up her books. Knowing that by now the rain would have soaked the plump seat of her bicycle, she decided to leave it where it was and escape from the rain by running from doorway to doorway. It was nearly ten o'clock, way past happy hour. As usual she had become so caught up in her work that she had forgotten to eat since lunchtime. She would make herself cheese on toast when she got back home. It was no good dropping by one of the many college student bars in the old city centre, as student bars don't serve food; at best, all she could get there would be a packet of crisps or some nuts.

As she skirted round the puddles and jumped over small rivulets of water rushing mindlessly down the drains to find their resting place in the black waters of the Cam, Lisa reflected on the opening

1

chapter of the book she had begun to write. Well, it was more of a diary really, but one never knew where a diary might lead. And anyway, it was a useful exercise to capture those interesting thoughts and bits of research that would otherwise become lost in a mountain of scribbled scraps of paper and post-it notes. Writing things down to get them out of oneself and onto the page, open for examination and the possibility of new interpretations, was meant to be a cathartic experience and heaven knows she could do with some healing right now. Sure, she knew how liberating it was to be independent, but it could also sometimes be a solitary and lonely existence being a student.

Living in Cambridge and being constantly surrounded by people and parties and never being quite alone, she was still, paradoxically, lonely at times. Night times to be precise. Night times when the libraries and the bars were closed and those people who were one half of a couple would seek out and snuggle up to the other part of themselves, sharing an affectionate or passionate embrace, coming together in those brief hours to become whole at last.

Lisa was thirty-three; gorgeous, American, and single. From the perspective of an undergraduate she was kind of old to be studying at Cambridge, but these days no university is deemed truly inclusive unless it admits undergraduate and postgraduate students from every religious and geographical denomination. Even so, she was lucky to get in.

Cambridge doesn't take many Visiting Students, and Magdalene College, pronounced 'maudlin', didn't accept women at all until 1988. Yes, that's right, 1988, not 1888. This was quite a surprise to Lisa, too, when she heard it, and not much surprised her. Whilst doing her research and deciding whether to go to Oxford or

Cambridge she learned that historically Cambridge was an important trading centre, popularised by the Romans who built a garrison fort here. They also built one of the first wooden bridges which crossed the river right in the centre of town, just in the place where today the old iron bridge sits by the Quayside.

Lisa was fascinated to think that Cambridge University was established in the town in the thirteenth century, with 'town and gown' rivalries still common even until the middle of the last century. Now, the University comprises thirty-one different colleges with Peterhouse being the oldest, founded in 1284, and Robinson the youngest, as it was only established in 1981. Magdalene was founded in 1542, so it took more than four hundred years for Magdalene to allow women scholars through its portals. Sometimes change happens slowly in England. Lisa loved the thought that by studying in Cambridge she would become a part of living history. Her link to the past was something that she felt passionate about. After all, if it wasn't for the past, she wouldn't have come here at all.

So now here she was, at one of the most breathtakingly beautiful places in England, doing postgraduate research in the sociology and psychology of relationships, trying to understand and untangle the dynamics of the things that make us who we are.

At an age that would once have been considered middle-aged, Lisa had done her fair share of travelling and as she would readily admit to her friends, had successfully lurched from one bad relationship to another. Unlike Greta Garbo, she hadn't wanted to be alone and being with someone she even half fancied had seemed somehow preferable to being single.

Boy, what a mistake that had been; trying to become the perfect girlfriend and morphing into someone else's expectations of herself, rather than finding out who she really was and what she really wanted out of life.   So now she had decided to spend some time getting to know herself before she invested any more time in getting to know someone else.   Thinking about it, she reckoned that she'd avoided getting to know the real Lisa for a long time. She'd been scared that there was something wrong with her, scared that she was somehow rotten at the core, so she ran away from herself.   She'd been frightened that she wouldn't like the person she was inside, terrified that underneath her layers of coping strategies, which kept her safe and warm like so many jumpers from a charity shop, that she really was as worthless as she sometimes felt.

But both her history and her future had brought her here to Cambridge, trying to learn more about herself and the legacy of madness that her family have given her; her final attempt to unravel and understand the past like a kitten chasing a ball of wool.

Not exactly black, but not exactly white either, Lisa knew what it's like to be displaced, living some kind of half-life; not fitting in with the rest of society and yet somehow having to find her place within it.   A curious combination of being on the outside looking in and yet also being on the inside looking out at the same time.   The paradox of multiple perspectives.   She had often been told that she resembled her great, great, great, great grandmother; that they shared the same green eyes and pale coffee latte colouring. According to one of her aunts she had the same long limbs and dancer's body.   Lithe, taught and strong.   A lucky inheritance. Although not everything that Lisa had inherited from her was quite so fortunate.

4

Does every family have its secrets? Stories told in hushed voices that are whispered down the generations through the gossamer curtain of time. Lisa had first heard her family story sitting on her grandmother's knee years before she learned to read. The 'family secret'. The skeleton in the closet shared only between the women: the mothers, daughters and sisters, aunts and cousins. A story passed down to each of them as a warning.

The tale you are about to hear is one of passion and intrigue, of greed and guilt, of cold-blooded murder and of utter ruthlessness. It is a story of grief and survival, of forbidden love and of the darkness of revenge. But it is also a love story. A tale of compassion and forgiveness, and ultimately, of triumph over adversity. It is a story of hope, of a journey to find someone with whom you can truly be yourself. If you want an uplifting tale of tenderness and of the healing power of love and touch you will find it here. If you want to know that love really can conquer all, you will also find that lesson here. If you are looking for something, but you are not quite sure what, or if you are looking for someone but you are not quite sure who, read on.

"Reader, I married him", said Jane Eyre in one of the most famous lines of English romantic literature. Yes Jane, indeed you did marry him. But someone else got there before you, and she was Lisa's great, great, great, great grandmother.

This is the story of the first Mrs Rochester. The real story. Not the convenient version that Charlotte Brontë wrote for Jane Eyre, but the story of what really happened. Everyone, probably you included, believes that Mr Rochester's first wife was mad. But the real story is very different. Very different indeed. Lisa only had one picture of her. A miniature portrait commissioned for her wedding day. That fateful union with Mr Edward Fairfax Rochester. She seems happy enough behind the glass, dewy eyed in love with no hint of fear or the insanity that was to come. According to family history there were no portraits after that time. It wouldn't have been advisable. She was meant to be dead after all.

Chapter 2

The Mason family were wealthy plantation owners on a small island in the West Indies set in the warm waters and sweet, balmy air of the Caribbean. Sugar cane was a good business to be in and the family Estate covered much of the land that wasn't too sandy to farm. Old Mr Mason, being well used to having his own way, became enamoured with one of the prettiest and palest of his Jamaican Creole slave girls who bore him three beautiful daughters, viewing the relationship as a way of advancing her own circumstances. Besides, it wasn't as if she had any choice in the matter. As a slave, she was legally his property, to do with as he pleased. But she reasoned that she might as well live as his mistress half way up the hill, near the big house, as his whore down in the slave village where younger and prettier girls would always be his temptation.

After old Mr Mason's first wife died, he moved his mistress up to the big house and brought her daughters up as his own. As white. Despite their mixed heritage, with their light skin and Caucasian features, it was an easy deception. When the Abolition of Slavery was passed on the 1ˢᵗ of August 1834 he freed them and their mother promising her marriage, a small detail he never actually achieved, although it was always assumed that it was something he had really meant to do.

Determined to better himself socially, old Mr Mason wooed a certain Mr Rochester whom he had met in Spanish Town, Jamaica. Mr Rochester was an English gentleman; a landowner from the north Shires who had two sons, both of whom were unmarried and therefore not only in want of a

7

wife, but the younger of the two, Mr Edward Fairfax Rochester, was also in want of a fortune, inheriting, as he did, nothing from his father's Estate but the meagre living of the Rectory.

Not immune to the fact that his fortune was a powerful incentive, Mr Mason encouraged a liaison between Edward Rochester and his eldest daughter. Antoinetta Bertha Mason was considered quite a beauty with skin the colour of lightly burnt sugar, something old Mr Mason was quite proud of, considering how he had made his money. Antoinetta, not yet twenty, was a wilful and headstrong girl. Encouraged by her father to indulge her passionate disposition, she was naturally excited by the promise of a new life in English society, of which she imagined much.

They were quickly married. Mr Rochester fancied himself in love, and he delighted in her daredevil, and completely inappropriate, habit of riding bareback on the sand at sundown, galloping through the shallow breakers on the beach and across the golden dunes in the fading evening light, after which they would fall into each other's arms. In a wooden lodge specially built for the purpose, warmed by the Caribbean winds they were free to indulge their ardour for each other under the enveloping blanket of darkness.

But their passion was short-lived. Finding it difficult to control her exuberant nature, exhausted by her constant questioning regarding their new life in England and the date of their arrival to it, Mr Rochester involved himself in the running of the Estate and avoided his new wife during the day at least. When she fell pregnant after barely two months of marriage, her constant sickness was a welcome excuse to leave her with her mother and sisters for company in another part of the house. When the baby was born Mr Rochester was humiliated and ashamed to see a cocoa coloured creature with a short, flat nose and curly, ebony black hair. Although Antoinetta protested her innocence, cried continually and tried to cling to him, there was no doubt in his mind that the bastard was not his. When it died three months later he was not sorry. His wife repulsed him and the Estate bored him. He left for Spanish Town, Jamaica, and did not return for five years.

After old Mr Mason died his son and heir by his first wife succeeded him. Richard Mason was a fair man but somewhat weak and rather too inclined to rely on the advice and opinions of others. Under his tutelage the Estate stumbled on for a while, lurching drunkenly from one crisis to another until land had to be sold. Mr Rochester returned to find the accounts in disarray and his wife penniless. However, having invested her dowry wisely and having quite by chance recently inherited his father's Thornfield Estate after the untimely death of his elder brother, Edward Fairfax Rochester resolved to leave the prison shores of the island and return to his beloved England. He had grown tired of the Caribbean and longed for the chill of sharp English frosts to soothe his equally cold heart. Learning that he had been duped into marrying the illegitimate daughter of a union between an ill-educated man and his slave, only strengthened his resolve to leave, never to return.

Trunks were packed and dispatched ahead to the Shire with strict instructions that they were not, under any circumstances, to be opened before the Master's arrival. Rather than excitement at her sudden departure for England Antoinetta resented being torn from her family by an estranged husband she no longer knew and no longer liked, let alone loved.   Her anger and violent outbursts of temper, driven by grief for the loss of her father and her unacknowledged child, only served to revolt Mr Rochester further.   Once on the boat he sedated her often with those opiate drugs so readily available to him in Spanish Town and by the time they landed in England he had made his wife an addict.

Upon arrival on the beloved shores of his England, Mr Rochester smuggled his insentient wife into Thornfield Hall where he secreted her on the third floor under the watchful gaze of Grace Poole, whom he had specially engaged for the task.   Easily controlled by her cravings for the drugs she had become so dependent on, Antoinetta surrendered to the will of her husband and resigned herself to a life of solitude and the long, harsh English winters so totally devoid of the temperate weather and sandy beaches of home.

To reduce the likelihood of escape still further Mr Rochester burned her shoes and boots on a pyre in the grounds, watching the smoke and flames snake into the sky before departing for the playing fields of Europe, where, like Lord Byron before him, he could both please himself and lose himself.   In European society, a man was of interest purely for his fortune or his talent and difficult questions were rarely asked.   He returned periodically only when matters on the Estate demanded it.   Antoinetta sometimes watched his

arrival and departure through her windows, but she had no
desire to engage with him, nor he with her.

By day, she was locked in a prison not of her own making.
Incarcerated, buried, interred; dead to all the world.   A life
unlived, a still life. Trapped in time, silent and forgotten. But
there were moments when she could no longer be silent, when
grief for all things lost overwhelmed her.   Jane Eyre heard her
cries, but even she, imaginative as she was, could not have
imagined the depth of Antoinetta's despair.

Chapter 3

Lisa spent the weekend thinking about relationships. Some time ago she had submitted an abstract to a conference about the ways that the dynamics of a romantic relationship change over time. Her abstract, which was essentially a short précis of her ideas and arguments had been accepted and now she had to write the full paper that would be included in the conference proceedings. She wanted to make her writing a personal narrative, almost like writing a letter to a friend. Not the usual way of academic writing, but that was one of the great things about the annual British Academy of Management conference; at BAM every member has a voice and there seems to be a Special Interest Group, a SIG, to support everyone in their own way. In academia there has been an ongoing 'relevance/rigour' debate that has raged for many years. Some people feel that the most important thing about academic research is that it's rigorously and scrupulously done, regardless of whether it's actually of any use to anyone! The other camp, who feel just as passionately, consider that unless academic research has a practical application for the practitioner in the real world, that the research is simply 'academic' in the sense of being an utterly pointless exercise.

Whilst Lisa recognised that a piece of research could be beautiful in the academic rigour of its design and execution, she also felt very strongly that it should be relevant, practical, applicable and readily understood by those people it would benefit most. She wanted her work and her writing to be both relevant and rigorous. Not easy in a world where academics and practitioners seem to speak two completely different languages and where very often, neither can fully understand the other. Lisa enjoyed having an idea in her mind and just letting thoughts about it drift in and out of her head. She knew quite a lot about relationships already, having had so many of them; some long, some short, some good and some bad. It occurred to her that there are many different kinds of relationships and if we are lucky and live a full life, we can experience the subtle colours of many of them. Even the unhealthy ones, she thought, can teach us something.

Despite having written and submitted the abstract, she really had no idea where to start writing. She wanted something catchy and interesting. The thought occurred to her to start at the beginning, but she wasn't quite sure where that was. So she let that thought ride and went to work, walking through the busy afternoon streets to Scudamore's punting station on the Quayside. Even as a mature post graduate student, without a scholarship, she was, by definition, somewhat short on both earnings and disposable income, so she combined people watching with making what little money she could after lectures and her supervision meetings were over. By acting as a chauffeur on the punts which glide full and then rest empty on the river Cam that meanders its way through the heart of the city behind and between the colleges, Lisa could observe the dynamics of myriad relationships over the course of a day. Families, friends, lovers, professional colleagues and strangers, she had seen them all. Each one fascinating in its own way, Lisa could remember a thousand scenes in the imagination of her mind; memories formed in moments that might last a lifetime.

She loved the slow tranquil elegance of the punts. Furnished with covered foam cushions and striped woollen blankets, the punts became beds or sofas, workhorses that didn't need feeding, ready and willing to accommodate the day's tourists. Sometimes they were narrow cosy single beds, perfect for intimate couples oblivious to the rest of the world as it slid slowly by next to them. Sometimes they were wide double beds, big enough for robust families on noisy picnics, eating, drinking, bickering and laughing on the water. Sometimes they were settees, replete with Japanese sightseers each with at least one expensive camera, cool shades and a sunhat. Lisa liked the Americans best. Excited to be in a place steeped in history and generous with their tips, they reminded her of home and she often gave them private tours of the University colleges in exchange for supper and some company.

The weekend was largely uneventful, except for a rather fat nine year old who insisted on falling into the Cam, despite warnings about the dangers of standing up in the punt and trying to touch the ceilings of each of the many bridges that the river tour took them under. He had been an accident waiting to happen and somewhat predictably he sank rather than floated. As she hauled him out of the water and then climbed back into the punt dripping wet, Lisa wished that she had remembered to put a bra on; her nipples were clearly visible through her tee shirt and the kid's father was looking at them. It was obviously time to go home and change.

Chapter 4

The third floor of the Hall, upon which Antoinetta was held prisoner, had, of course, many more than the three rooms that contained her. In preparation for her arrival Mr Rochester cordoned off a wing of the house to accommodate his secret and his shame; spreading rumours of ghosts and ghouls to keep the servants away. Food, coal and water were carried up narrow wooden staircases and along dimly lit passageways to be quickly deposited by kitchen and scullery maids too terrified to linger. They never made the journey alone; almost petrified by the tales of phantoms and the paranormal. When Mrs Poole entered the kitchens, they looked away.

Grace Poole. A name that suggests elegance and elevation. A name that dances across the pages of life. A gift from God. The stark reality of Grace Poole, however, could not be further from the description suggested by her name. A woman of uncertain age and uncertain background, she had answered Mr Rochester's advertisement some ten years earlier. A decision she had not regretted for even a second; to the contrary, her new position suited her purpose very well. Although at some point in her life she may have been a pretty girl, with long brown hair and a neat figure, any memory of that existence had been lost over time. Now her long hair was grey, almost white, tied back severely in a tightly knotted bun, and her face was as hard and sharp as the grey stone of the Hall itself. Having risen from scullery maid to wet nurse by virtue of an unfortunate pregnancy many years ago courtesy of the Master of a house in a neighbouring county, her history was, at best, forgotten.

Despite never having married and therefore technically a spinster, Grace called herself 'Mrs' Poole, thereby affording herself a dignity in life that had in reality thus far eluded her. As she was neither governess nor nanny, no family would retain or retire her so she had to find employment where she could. Years before she had taken advantage of her situation and engaged in some wet nursing after her bastard baby had died. In fact, truth be told, she had smothered it herself soon after it was born, viewing it as a nuisance she could turn into a job opportunity. A small, whining little thing totally dependent on her, she had felt nothing but relief at its passing, and, taking the money that was paid for her inconvenience, had bought herself a wedding ring. Eventually, after some years, like Jane Eyre who followed her, good fortune found her a new position at Thornfield.

Mr Rochester paid her well for her silence; another secret she found easy to keep. She hid the money in a leather purse under her mattress, and at night, lying upon it, she dreamt of leaving this employ and buying a small house in Plymouth where she could retain some girls who, with a roof over their head and food in their bellies, would happily do the bidding of visiting sailors for the right price. But houses, even small ones, cost money so she supplemented her income by pawning Antoinetta's jewellery and trinkets. Taking only those things she thought her charge would not miss, over the years she slowly stole away the memories of Antoinetta's life.

When Antoinetta was free from the physical torment of her cravings for the opiates so readily supplied by her husband via the willing auspices of Grace Poole, she lived her life in a world of fractured reality where it wasn't clear to her what was real and what she only imagined. Days, weeks and sometimes months would pass with no marker of time inside the rooms within which she lived her solitary existence. Only the changing colours of the landscapes outside her windows gave any clues as to the passage of time and those seasons that so governed the lives of the workers on the Estate. It was to be almost ten years before she could find a way to escape her prison and her jailor.

Ten years. Ten long years. Although after a while Antoinetta hardly felt the passing of time. She lived only in the moment, for the moment, having decided many years ago that the only way to survive her torture and imprisonment was to take one breath at a time. She tried not to look back to her life as it had been, as that filled her empty heart with regret and sorrow. Neither did she look forward to her future, because if ever she did, there was nothing there. Before sleep she often prayed she would not wake; would not live to see another day. But it was not to be and she could only assume that God had a plan for her. On those days when she was not fighting her cravings she often filled her time with sewing and painting, with attending to her toilette and by writing letters to her brother and her sisters, letters that Grace Poole never sent. On other days she played a game with herself. Sitting in front of her dressing table, she would talk to her reflection in the mirror. Speaking in her native tongue rather than the stilted English that even Grace Poole would have understood, her jailor thought her deranged and speaking in tongues. She reported Antoinetta's apparent madness to her estranged husband, who, with the certainty of previous conversations with the medical profession of the time, remained convinced that Antoinetta was not just mad, but incurably so.

Antoinetta surveyed her room. The large bedroom housed an impressive fireplace, a grand oak four-poster bed, replete with heavy burgundy and gold curtains which, when drawn, kept Antoinetta warm and gave her a sense of secure enclosure. Outside the curtains was a world she did not wish to be a part of. In her bed she felt safe, if only for a short while. An inlaid ebony wooden chest of drawers stood at the foot of her sanctuary, a green velvet George IV rosewood chaise held court in one corner, while a willow rocking chair sat waiting patiently for her by the fire. In the long winter months it comforted her, in the summer months Grace Poole moved it allowing her to repose by the window overlooking the courtyard and stables. The voluptuous burgundy and gold drapes of the silk lined curtains of her windows were perfectly matched by the tapestries on the bed which, once drawn, kept the heat in and the nightmares of the flickering candles out.

Her dressing room held four wardrobes of Caribbean clothes, the majority of which were wholly unsuitable for a life in England. A small wash stand nestled in the corner and a large mirror sat above an equally large dressing table adorned with jewellery boxes, trinkets, brushes, hairpins and those other items so essential to a lady's toilette. Antoinetta's day room overlooked some of the Hall's kitchen gardens and fields of the Estate. It was a cosy room, containing a writing desk fully stocked with papers and ink, a second rocking chair, watercolour paints, an easel, two rather uncomfortable Regency sofas and a pair of matching chairs. It was here that

Mrs Rochester spent her time writing, sewing, drawing and imagining the lives of those servants she watched going about their daily business and growing older through her windows.

There was one servant in particular she had watched with interest grow from a boy to a man; noticed how the awkwardness of youth had been replaced by a calm self-confidence. A lanky skeleton transforming in front of her eyes to become the frame of a muscular young man, ready to take his place on the Estate and in the world. She did not know his name, only that he was often to be seen with the horses and in the stable courtyard. Antoinetta watched him often, noted his work clothes and admired his livery. She grieved when she saw him drive a carriage away from the Hall and waited impatiently for his return. She imagined a life for him and fantasised imaginary conversations when the wind carried wisps of his voice to her through her open windows. She often wondered how it would feel to fold herself into his strong and muscular arms. After nearly ten years she longed to be touched. Longed to be held, longed to be kissed and made to feel like a woman again. She pleaded with God for one more kiss before dying. One moment of passion; she asked for nothing more. Just one kiss. The passionate embrace of a passing stranger to gently stroke her hair and trace the contours of her face with his fingers. But much as she longed to be touched in the frequent fantasies of her mind, Antoinetta dismissed her thoughts and kept her silence. Grace Poole knew nothing of the moments that Antoinetta imagined for herself.

Grace Poole drank gin and water. A mother's ruin. Antoinetta learned that a few drops of the drugs that Mr

Rochester used to subdue her dropped inconspicuously into the glass when Grace was otherwise occupied would cause a combination that sent Grace into a stupor from which she could not be roused.   As Grace Poole twitched and snorted her way through unconsciousness, Antoinetta stole the house keys from her jailor and set herself free.   At first tentative, unsure of herself and terrified of discovery, under the comforting widow's veil of black, by night she roamed the corridors and galleries of Thornfield Hall like a feral cat, barefoot and silent as the crypt she was entombed in.   While the servants were asleep, she was finally mistress of the house and she knew every inch of it, every smell and every creaking floorboard.   Every hidden door and servants' passageway. Every hiding place and every sanctuary.   Every bedroom and everything in each one.   Silent, unseen and unheard, she could find her way with ease in the darkness.   Moving swiftly along the corridors and narrow passageways that kept the servants invisible to polite society, she had a picture of the house and its internal runways within her head and could follow it like a map.

By moonlight the house was her playground.   Sometimes at night Antoinetta would slip off to the stables to be with the horses, to feel their gentle strength and be warmed by their soft hot breath against her skin.   They didn't judge her.   They didn't flinch from her touch or look away when she approached them.   Grace Poole looked at her with pity and disdain.   Her estranged husband looked at her with loathing and disgust.   Only the horses and Pilot the dog were ever pleased to see her.

Chapter 5

Tired, Lisa saved her work onto her student account and then out of habit backed it up on her memory stick before shutting down the computer. Her watch said nine thirty. It was Easter full term and the main university library, known simply as the UL, would soon be closing for the night. She had been lost in her thoughts of Antoinetta and Mr Rochester at the beginning of their relationship, when they were newly married; each in the other's thrall, lost in the obsession of infatuation when we see our partners as we want them to appear rather than as they really are.

Lisa knew from her research that it is now well recognised within psychology that the dynamics of a couple's relationship will change over time. The beginning of a new, sexually intimate relationship is called 'the honeymoon' period. In this stage, a couple is 'falling in love' and desperate to get to know each other better, in every sense. Everything about the other person is as yet unknown. Every meeting and every conversation is exciting and the sex between the couple is often as intoxicating as it is all consuming. In the throes of passion, those character traits which drive you almost crazy with frustration later on in the relationship are either viewed as strengths or are ignored completely. It's almost as if the couple are addicted to each other. In fact, research shows that the physiological changes that occur within the body, like changes in blood chemistry and distorted thought patterns, such as the disregard of obvious risks, are very similar to those changes that occur when someone takes mood-altering drugs.

However, this level of energy, this excitement, cannot and does not last. Within a year to eighteen months the relationship will change and the honeymoon period will be over. In unhealthy relationships, some couples try to rekindle the heady excitement and passion of those first intoxicating months by splitting up, parting and restarting the relationship. As a short-term strategy, this can often be quite successful, but ultimately, unless the couple can progress to the next stage of a relationship together, their union is doomed to failure. Some people are even addicted to passion itself, doing their best to stay permanently in the honeymoon period. Such people will move from one relationship to the next, never able to sustain a relationship for longer than two years at most.

So what happens after the honeymoon period is over? As Lisa had never got beyond it herself in any of her previous relationships, she wasn't quite sure. According to the theory, stage two, which occurs after the end of the honeymoon period and up to approximately year five of a relationship, involves nesting and making a home. It's all about defining the roles within the relationship and developing the strategies a couple needs to become truly compatible; learning to live with each other in the longer term. This is the commitment stage where couples who have decided to stay together often also decide to have children. Frequently, so tired from parenting, unless the people in such a partnership make a conscious effort to take the time to nurture each other and the relationship, they hardly seem to notice the fact that the lust and passion that they used to share has dwindled.

The third stage, which tends to occur between six and ten years of the relationship, is characterised by the establishment of customs and traditions, such as Christmas and birthday rituals, and by building on, and sharing, everything that the relationship has to offer, both emotionally and financially. By now a couple will have settled into a comfortable routine and will have learned how to deal with any conflict within the relationship.

Lisa wondered about the famous 'seven year itch' which logic suggested would usually occur within this stage. Did one part of a couple always feel the need to stray or explore other opportunities in approximately the seventh year, or could it sometimes happen within years nine or ten? What differentiated those people who strayed compared to those who didn't? What was it they were searching for? Lost passion perhaps? Excitement? What was there to guarantee that by ending their current relationship and returning to stage one, they wouldn't get itchy feet in another seven years?

In healthy relationships, stage four, which occurs approximately between years eleven and twenty-five, is likely to be an ongoing continuation of stage three. But even then, the individuals within the relationship may well experience some kind of mid-life crisis in which they begin to question the meaning and importance of the relationship, or even, sometimes, the meaning of life itself. Lisa thought that perhaps this was the most dangerous stage of a couple's relationship. Historically, a couple might well have stayed together, 'for the sake of the children', but social mores and individual expectations have changed. In the twenty-first century people now seem to expect to be fulfilled within their most personal relationship, and living an unhappy life, or a life as best friends rather than as passionate lovers, is no longer an acceptable option for many people. This means that, potentially, within stage four, a couple may split up and form a new relationship and by so doing, return to stage one with their new partner.

The fifth and final stage of relationships happens after approximately twenty-five years. This stage marks an acceptance of the status quo between the couple and there is often a renewal of commitment to the relationship. Couples are usually more financially secure and, free from the stress of contraception and the pressure and responsibility of raising children, there is an opportunity to make more time for each other. This tends to be the time when grandchildren appear within the relationship and the couple become concerned, individually and as a partnership, with leaving a legacy for future generations.

Of course, Lisa realised that none of these stages are set in stone, and the timescales are at best only approximations. It seemed a shame that at thirty-three she had never progressed beyond stage one, but then again, perhaps it was better to be single and happy without the debris of a fractured family behind her, than to be in an unhappy relationship just so that she was not on her own. She had never met anyone she had wanted to settle down with who had seemed to want to settle down with her at the same time. Perhaps she would, one day.

Lisa left the UL, walking across the impressive black and white marble entrance hall and skipping down the steps outside. She always thought that it was a rather incongruous building; built in the 1930s, its plain dull brick façade was in stark contrast to the magnificence within and the beauty of its hidden treasures. As one of the country's six Deposit Libraries, it had the right to request a complimentary copy of every book published within the United Kingdom, although having run out of space some years ago, it rarely executed that right. Neither did the Bodleian in Oxford, although the British Library seemed to have a copy of just about everything, even if requesting it via inter-library loans necessitated a long wait. It would be such a shame, she thought, if progress meant that all books in the future would only be available in digital format. She loved the smell and feel of books and manuscripts, loved to ponder who had studied the same passages before her looking for meaning, and was always curious to know, although she never would of course, which students had broken library rules by writing their own notes or comments in the margins.

Opposite the UL, walking along The Backs, past the rear views of some of the oldest university colleges, Lisa continued to think about the passion of new relationships.   Does passion always dissipate over time, evaporating like breath in a frost.   Or rather, do the dynamics of passion simply change over time and transform into something emotionally stronger and deeper?   Lisa wondered about the passion between Mr Rochester and Antoinetta and the nature of their relationship.   They had met and married in the late 1830s after the Abolition of Slavery Act of 1833.   A very different time.   A time when there were different expectations of marriage.   A time when marriage was a business transaction; a partnership for life, with or without love.   With or without passion.   They had something in common she thought, herself and Antoinetta; they were both stuck at stage one.

As she walked, now along the narrow cobbled streets of central Cambridge, Lisa considered what she knew about Antoinetta's husband, Edward Fairfax Rochester.   What kind of a man was he? Was he drawn to Antoinetta's passionate nature in the same way that he would be drawn to a wild stallion?   Drawn to her because of his desire to conquer her and break her spirit, to bend her to his will?   It was true that he liked women to stand up to him; women who weren't afraid of him.   After all, that was one of the things he liked about Jane Eyre.   But Antoinetta Bertha Mason wasn't Jane Eyre.   Indulged by her parents she was a passionate and headstrong woman and Mr Rochester found that he couldn't tame her.   If he couldn't control her and no longer loved her, was it really so acceptable to dismiss her grief and craving for affection as hysteria and lock her up?   To take her away from her family and incarcerate her upstairs for ten years while he found comfort in the arms of other women?

Chapter 6

In his early thirties, John was tall and broad shouldered with slim hips, a rider's thighs and strong powerful arms, tanned from the long summers of working outside. With his dark good looks, chestnut eyes and the body of a natural athlete, he was never short of female company, should he want it. Amongst the womenfolk, from the maids in the house and the farmers' wives on the Estate to the daughters of the town's tradesmen, John was popular and well liked. With a ready smile and a kind nature, John was respected for the way he handled the horses and the way he handled himself. In town and on the Estate he was known as John, the Coachman from Thornfield. His father had been old Mr Rochester's coachman before him and following in his father's footsteps, he took up his first position as stable boy at twelve, groom at fifteen and finally as coachman at twenty-one when his father was too old and his hands too crooked and bent with arthritis, from a lifetime of being rained upon, to manage the carriage driving reins and whip any longer.

Lean and muscular from a lifetime's work riding and grooming the horses, if it wasn't for his brown and tan work clothes, from a distance you would almost think that it was Mr Rochester himself striding across the fields and round the Estate. Of similar height and build, there were differences between John and Edward Rochester of course, not least the way each preferred to master the young horses that would eventually take their place either under saddle or between the shafts of one of Mr Rochester's many carriages. Edward Fairfax Rochester, proud and domineering, would break a horse to his will, forcing it to yield to his hand and obey him.

27

John would spend time with each youngster, getting to know them, watching them move and learning their moods so they wanted to please him and immediately did as he asked, without force or subjugation, willingly yielding to his every request.

A gifted healer, John would gently but firmly massage his horses, soothing their tired muscles after a days hunting or carriage work. A safe pair of hands, never rough and never raised in anger, the horses would lean into his touch, their bottom lips sagging and drooping downwards as they became more and more relaxed under the hypnotic spell of his strong and rhythmic strokes. They trusted him implicitly and watched his every move with patient eyes, knowing their place on the Estate as John knew his. This life was all of their experience, and, like the man who touched them so expertly, they accepted it without question.

With his father's job on the Estate, John inherited the use of Coachman's Cottage. Plainly decorated, John had not altered it since his mother and father had retired from service and been moved to another tied dwelling some years before. It suited him well, although at five minutes walk from the stable block, he sometimes slept in the hay loft above the horses if one of them had a slight chill or colic and might need his attention.

On one such night, as the moonlight streamed blue through the open hayloft doors, with the sweet smell of summer on the breeze, he was woken by a whicker and the gentle stamping of hooves below as one of his charges pawed the ground in greeting. Looking down from his makeshift bed of hay and blankets he saw a long haired and dark skinned girl in the stable below, tenderly stroking the nose of Mesrour, the Master's magnificent black stallion. Barefoot, the gold rings on her toes caught the moonlight, slightly startling the horse. An exotic gypsy, an ethereal spectre, dressed only in white undergarments, she blew gently up the stallion's nose so he could smell her scent. It calmed the startled steed, as John knew that it would, and he dropped his glossy black head to lick at her hand. She toyed for a moment with his bushy black forelock and small neat ears before laughing playfully as he licked at her wrist some more. Slipping her left hand through the mane by his withers, with the agility of a cat she vaulted onto the stallion's broad gleaming back. Leaning forwards to whisper in his ear, her long dark curly hair tangled with the stallion's mane so that John could not see where her hair ended and the horse began.

He watched for a few moments as she sat still and silent, stroking her mount's smooth ebony neck while the magnificent animal bent his head and nibbled at sweet smelling hay. Sitting astride, her long limbs hanging loosely down the horse's sides, she continued to lean forwards, stroking his ears and whispering into them. John thought that she was the most breathtakingly beautiful woman he had ever seen; a dusky beauty, slim and delicate, exotic and mysterious. As he continued to watch, safe in his eerie above, from nowhere, large silent tears slowly slid down her face and quiet sobs racked her body. Oblivious to his presence and blind from her tears she did not notice as John dropped down from the hay loft above her and onto the floor. Landing lightly on the straw he walked across the stable, reached up and caught her tiny wrist easily in his hand. Startled, she

29

gasped in surprise, twisting her arm in his grasp and John found himself looking into her feral green eyes. Like a young colt, he saw not wilfulness staring back at him but fear and misunderstanding. Relaxing his grip and letting her free from his grasp so as not to frighten her further, they both knew she could not escape past him and flee into the night.

Looking through her tears and deep into her eyes, John felt her gaze burning deeply into his soul, pleading with him to set back the clock of time, begging for her liberty, to be set free into the night from whence she'd come. He stood his ground as she did hers. Neither moved a muscle. Two statues in the moonlight, each searching for answers in the eyes of the other. Taking one step back to give her space to dismount he offered his hand. She took it and, bending her right knee to lift her leg over the neck of her mount, slipped silently and neatly to the ground in front of him. In one smooth movement he caught her as she landed on the straw. With one hand holding hers and his other hand around her waist to balance her descent, they were caught for a fleeting moment in a silent embrace. Had she asked him now, he would have let her go; would have freed her back into the night. Sensing this, instead of pulling away from him, she took a step closer and looking up in to his eyes, pushed her body against his broad muscular chest, offering herself up to whatever might be his will. Next to him, how small and delicate she seemed; a wounded bird devoid of flight, caught in his arms as a thrush in the hedge. As she continued to look up, John bent his head to hers and in the smoothness of motion that only lovers can share, their lips met in a first intimate embrace.

It was a kiss like neither had experienced before. Two statues again, a lifetime in a moment. A lifetime she had imagined and prayed for so many times. In kissing his gypsy for the first time, John learned everything he needed to know about her; knew instinctively how much she wanted him and how tenderly and willingly she would inevitably submit. Slowly they explored each other. Their kisses gentle and hesitant at first, growing more passionate. Then, gentle once again, like the ebb and flow of the surf on a warm Caribbean beach. Not silent, they spoke the language of lovers; involuntary sighs breaking the stillness of the night as waves lap at the shore. John felt her hunger and her passion as she leant into him, supple and compliant in the strong arms he wrapped around her. Lost in each other, they were lost in time.

John smelt of horse liniment and leather. A smell that reminded her of home. After ten years of cruel confinement the most desperate and deepest desire of her heart was to escape from this world and go home. This man's smell and his touch transported her there and she lost herself completely in his warm embrace, a willing participant in their dance of desire. Fully clothed, they were intimate strangers. Known and yet unknown. John wanted to hold her to him and wrap her in his arms, but instead he gently pushed her away so he could examine her in the moonlight. Her gaze met his, unafraid but confused. Did he not want her? John drank in the sight of her and devoured her with his eyes. Yes, he wanted her. He had never wanted anything as much.

It was a moment in time, which, although it seemed as if it would last forever, he knew would pass too soon. John was sure that this was no dream, but neither somehow did it seem real. He pulled her to him and kissed her once again. No hesitation this time. No confusion. No questions. No wasted seconds. Just passion. The place where physical desire and emotion meet. He drowned in her as she did in him. Two souls taking flight and soaring aloft like eagles hunting in dawn's early light, circling each other in the smooth dance of partnership, riding the rising thermals upwards. In that moment, the night seemed endless. Their first kisses opening a window in time the gypsy prayed would last forever. A desperate wish. Foolish in its naivety. Laying fully clothed where they had fallen into each other's arms on the straw, when they heard the church clock strike five John felt her stiffen against him. She gasped and pulled herself from his embrace. Still silent, and without yet having spoken a word, she pulled back from him and with one more teasing kiss, ran off into the day.

If it were not for the fact that he could smell the gypsy on his clothes and taste her on his lips, John would have sworn that his encounter the previous night had been a dream. He spent the day working in and around the stables as usual, commanding the under coachmen, exercising the horses in the Estate fields, tending to splints and sprains on horses' legs and making running repairs to the leather harness neatly stored on pegs and wooden saddle racks in the tack room. Twice he felt as though he saw a glimpse of his mysterious gypsy, but when he looked at the place he imagined seeing her, there was nothing. Perhaps he was going mad, or perhaps he was seeing what he was desperate to see? He shook his head and shook off his thoughts, forcing himself to focus on the task at hand. The night before seemed a lifetime away.

Chapter 7

Lisa woke early as the diagonal shafts of sunlight slid across her eyes from the small uncurtained window high on the wall to the right of her bed. Excited about the BAM conference paper she was about to write, words and sentences and fragments of paragraphs swirled around in her head like butterflies on a buddleia bush. As she lay warm and content, snuggled under her duvet, the morning sun hinted at the promise of a beautiful day.

Lisa's rooms were her sanctuary. As a mature, post-graduate student, she had arranged her own accommodation in one of the antique parts of the old city centre. A tiny medieval attic apartment, her rooms were modest, and as she wasn't in University Halls she didn't have a college 'bedder' who came in to clean her room once a week. She was quite happy to look after herself, however, and she had everything she needed. A comfortable single bed to one side of the room doubled as a sofa during the day. An oddly shaped wardrobe balanced somewhat precariously on the sloping floor. A cork notice board on the wall was strategically placed to hide a small damp patch and various assorted shelves worked in harmony with an L shaped desk in the corner by the window to create a comfortable working space that had one of the most beautiful views of the city that Cambridge had to offer. From this window, Lisa could see the bent and twisted roofs of Cambridge bronzed by the morning and evening light. She never tired of the romance of watching the rising and sinking sun dance over the city like a rumour, clinging to the wood, metal, stone and glass-like whispers on the wind caught up in the promise of the intellectual excitement that was the very essence of Cambridge.

Lisa would change the space she worked in either to suit her mood or deliberately to change her thinking. She had learned as a child that by changing her environment she could change the way that she thought about things. In this way she had joyfully discovered that the words subsequently flowing from her mind and through to her fingers would be magically transformed on the page, as if written by unseen hands. Within the enclave of the medieval history of her tiny rooms, she found that she wrote best in the mornings, after dawn's early light had licked her face awake, stroking her cheek as the birds began their chorus, transforming her silent world to nature's natural musical orchestra. Each day a gift, ripe with the promise of a future as yet unknown.

In Cambridge, the old university colleges, such as Trinity, founded in 1546 by King Henry VIII, St. John's and Christ's College, all had little nooks and crannies, hidden gardens and private seclusions, perfect for intellectual or spiritual contemplation, many of which you could access as a student. Having previously sought permission, and making sure that she was always friendly to the college porters, accompanied by a student she joyfully explored the university colleges, careful to always be respectful and delighting in finding new places to hide away and write. She particularly loved the Scholar's Garden in the grounds of Clare College. It was almost next to the field owned by King's College where she would sometimes stop and watch the cows graze. It amused her to think that she was living in probably the only city in Europe where cows happily munched grass just a hundred yards from the city centre.

To think through an essay, an academic paper or an article she had to write, Lisa would sometimes take a punt up river towards Grantchester Meadows. Of course, getting the punt up river and over the rollers from the Mill Pond next to the Garden House Hotel necessitated some help. Cambridge punts are solid wood, and it takes three people to haul one up and over the rollers whilst one person sits in the punt with the paddle. Every punt has a paddle; it's exactly what you need when your pole gets stuck fast in the mud of the Cam and you have to let go of it to avoid taking an early bath. Without a paddle as a brake, the momentum of the punt can keep you going a hundred yards in the wrong direction before you inadvertently bump someone or crash into the riverbank. On the way back down the river into the city, going down the rollers is good fun, a bit like a very short mini roller coaster ride. Then you paddle back to the side of the river and collect your pole from whichever friend has been kind enough to hold onto it for you.

To help her mind make more connections, see patterns between ideas or make sense of whichever research papers she had been reading, Lisa found the smoothness of punting, the repetitive and rhythmic circular motion of passing the pole through her hands and gently leaning her weight against it, strangely hypnotic and calming despite having permanently wet hands and wet feet from the dripping pole. She usually found that by the time she had moored the punt again, she was able to collect her thoughts and put them in some semblance of order. With her thoughts regarding how we become self-aware and the development of intimacy within relationships, Lisa had cycled around Cambridge, gone to work on the river, acted as tour guide, eaten, drunk and laughed, and sat in the Cambridge gardens in quiet contemplation for almost two months before she had finally pulled all the pieces of the jigsaw puzzle of intimacy together.

Lisa had given considerable thought to the process of developing self-awareness. Self-awareness is a necessary pre-requisite for developing emotional intimacy with yourself, and developing self-understanding and self-acceptance is a necessary pre-requisite for developing emotionally intimate and rich relationships with others. Becoming self-aware and emotionally intimate requires honesty and takes tremendous courage. Its purpose is not to learn to love someone else, but ultimately, to learn to love oneself.

Step one is motivation and it's probably the most difficult step of all. You've got to want to get to know yourself better, or at least be interested enough to consider it.

After more than thirty years in the world Lisa had come to the conclusion that people seek out experiences for two, quite different, reasons. There are those people who have experiences in order to find themselves, and those people who use experiences, such as drink, drugs, or sex, to achieve an altered physical or emotional state and avoid finding themselves. Usually because of fear. They are afraid that they won't like the person they are at their core. Worse still are those people who 'punish' others for liking them. These people don't like themselves and therefore they seem to believe that there must be something wrong with anyone who does like them. Any relationship which has this at its starting point is doomed to failure.

Step two is to accept your starting point. You need to recognise, acknowledge and accept that everything you have done and experienced in your life so far, every decision that you've ever taken, has made you into the person that you are today. Whether you like yourself or dislike yourself, this statement is true. So you might as well accept it. To deny it is to deny that your experiences and your reactions to them have made you who you are. So accept yourself, starting from now. Right now. Today.

Many people, even if they get past step one, become stuck at step two. Often because, in order to cope with what has happened to them in the past, they have become angry, either with themselves or with someone from their past. It is this anger that keeps them stuck and prevents them from moving on. Sometimes this anger goes unrecognised. Sometimes this anger is turned inwards. Turning anger in on oneself leads, eventually, to distress and illness. As a strategy for living a full and satisfied life it is necessary to let this anger go. We need to be able to forgive ourselves and others. After all, we are all doing the best we can, often in difficult and complex circumstances.

However, before you can find it within yourself to forgive either yourself or certain other people for those things which have hurt you in the past, it is imperative to learn more about yourself and other people. This is step three.

Step three is to use every opportunity to develop new insights and new understanding about yourself so that you can *be* yourself. Through the process of self-reflection, every experience that you have gives you the opportunity to get to know yourself better. How well do you know yourself already? Do you know for example, your strengths and weaknesses? And are your strengths those things that you really enjoy doing? How would other people describe you? Would they be the same words that you would use? What motivates or demotivates you? Are you aware of how you are feeling at each moment of the day? Are there times when you shut down your feelings and disconnect from the world and the people in it? Do you have strategies in place to lift your spirits and make you feel better about yourself if, for some reason, you are having a bad day?

Step three can be achieved at a number of levels. You can learn superficial things about yourself or very deep and meaningful things. Why is this important to me? is a good question to ask yourself. Even if you are scared about what the answer might be and what you might find out, you must be honest. If you are not, who are you really kidding? You are only deceiving yourself. Step three isn't a one-off. It takes time. It can take a whole lifetime as we never stop learning about ourselves. If we are not too self-absorbed, and if we are interested enough, we never stop learning about others. Only when you can understand and accept that none of us are perfect, that we all make mistakes at times even though we are doing the best we can, will you be able to forgive yourself and others. For many of us, that's a bridge we must cross before we can reach step four.

Step four involves deciding what you are going to do with this new information that you have about yourself. There may be some things about yourself that you would like to change. This is going to be particularly true if there are some things that you don't like very much. Sometimes step four may link you in to discovering meaning in your life or to your life's purpose. To change requires courage. On reflection, you may decide that you don't want to change, and that's ok too.

Step five, when you get that far, is relatively simple. It's this. Be happy. Be happy with who you are, with who you have become. By stage five you should know who you are, how your unique life story has contributed to making you the person that you are today. Learn to like yourself. Better than that, learn to really like yourself. And when you can learn to like yourself, with that self-understanding and self-acceptance you will be able to love yourself for who you really are.

It is worth pointing out here that the person you really are may not be the person that others see very often. That doesn't matter. It takes tremendous courage, not just to be who we really are, but to be brave enough to allow others to see, and share, our 'authentic' selves. You may chose to reserve the most personal parts of yourself for those people whom you love at home. Or, you may decide to live your life authentically and be who you really are and who you have the potential to be, in all areas of your life, at work, at home, and at play.

In this complex world, we each have many different roles to play, and sometimes, to avoid becoming vulnerable to those who might hurt us emotionally or psychologically, it is either easier or safer to hide who we really are under a veneer of professionalism. That's fine too. Just remember to find a space where you can relax and really be yourself, whether that's at home, in the garden, with close friends, when you are with your dog, or simply, when you are alone. Not everyone will be ready, but for those of you who are, good luck.

Lisa reviewed what she had written. A bit personal she thought, but not bad for a first draft. She would need to review it and tweak it a bit, but on the whole, she was quite pleased with herself. It was difficult writing for an unknown audience, but she hoped that what she had written would resonate and be helpful for some people at least, particularly if they wanted to learn about themselves and were finally ready to change certain things. Not everything. That would be unrealistic and probably destabilising. But some things. Those things about themselves that they had been carrying around for a long time and were ready to either change or finally let go. She knew from her own experience that it was important to speak from the heart. To be honest and to mean what you say so that the reader knows that you care and that your concern for them is truly compassionate regard.

"People don't care how much you know until they know how much you care".

She had learned that from the Samaritans.   It was good advice for writers as well as counsellors.

Chapter 8

Watching the daily business of the Estate through her windows, and desperate for a glimpse of the man to whom she had already given her heart, for Mrs Rochester, locked away on the third floor, the hours passed interminably slowly. A new governess had recently joined the household and her husband was at home. He drank into the night and retired late, demanding that his butler and valet also stayed up should he require their services for any small trifle that was his will. His wife thought the governess a plain little thing; young, insignificant and of little consequence. Possessing but one unfashionable, austere grey dress and spending her time either in the library or with Mr Rochester's ward, Adèle, she was easily overlooked.

Much as she disliked Grace Poole, Antoinetta knew better than to anger her jailor or give her any reason to chain her to the wall as had so often been the case in years past. A thin chain which allowed her to reach only her bed and its attendant commode. A chain which, however thin it might be, did not allow her to reach Grace's comatose form and take her keys whilst she slept. This chain anchored her more securely to the house than her dependence on her husband and the opiates he supplied ever could. Knowing from experience that while she was chained flight was impossible, Antoinetta had no choice but to wait, and to hope good fortune provided an early opportunity for freedom. But her guard was inexplicably restless and it was to be a week before she could escape again.

She spent her days and nights thinking about John. He had been everything she imagined, only his smell had surprised her. Much as she had prayed for a kiss, had begged the Lord to be touched by a real man just once more, she knew now that it was not enough. How could one brief meeting be enough with a man like John? She imagined their next meeting, lived many such occasions in her head, until in her fractured reality where night was day and day was night she almost believed that they had met many times. Sometimes, catching sight of him from her windows, each glimpse lit a fire of such powerful longing in her she was sure Grace Poole must notice. But Grace's head was full of her own concerns and if she saw the increased colour in Antoinetta's cheeks and the brightness of her eyes, she did not mention it. After so long she had little interest in her charge, save that of knowing the day and precise amount of her monthly wage, supplemented, of course, by those little trinkets she could pawn in the town on her occasional visits there.

May was warm that year. Spring had come early with pheasants laying their eggs under hedgerows and in the growing grasses of the meadows. Budding blossom nestled amongst sprouting green leaves offering the promise of new life and new possibilities. Each night of that week in the time between sleeping and waking John waited for his wild gypsy to come to him. Night after night he was disappointed. He knew not from whence she came, nor did he care. He just knew he was willing to wait for her, all night if necessary, and the following night, and the one after that. Asking after her on the Estate, his enquiries were met with shaken heads. Asking after the movements of itinerant Romanies in the town, he was again told that no-one had seen or heard of any traveller who matched her description. Only the strength of his memory and the passion he felt in his loins encouraged him to believe that he would, and must, see her again.

On the seventh night John once again set a bed of blankets in the hay loft above the stables. A light sleeper, he was woken by the scent of a woman and the whisper of promise on the wind. Still dressed in his tan work clothes and worn brown leather riding boots, John threw off his covers and raised himself to his knees, a swell of excited recognition rising in his stomach. But before he could stand, his barefoot princess had climbed the ladder to his eyrie and padded silently to his bed, settling herself like a cat, curled in his muscular arms. Lifting her head to look silently into his eyes, her lips once again met his and they locked in another exquisite embrace. This time, however, after their first kiss, the gypsy did not flee back from whence she had come. Instead, John smiled and explored her mouth with his own. He lifted her in his arms and, like the tendrils of the vines that follow the passage of the sun through the sky, wrapped them around her neat and delicate waist, pulling her on top of himself and pinning her to him. Then, in one smooth movement he rolled her over underneath him, so he was the master and she his willing servant.

Gently, slowly, tenderly, almost afraid that any sudden movements might scare their partner into flight, they found mutual pleasure in each other's company. Perfectly matched. Equal in every sense, one fitted the other like a glove and its hand. Antoinetta was so lost in the sensations of the moment; lips against lips, it was impossible to tell where her body ended and John's began. In the hours between sleeping and

43

waking they explored each other, each waiting for the signals of readiness from the other. Each healing their partner through the gift of touch and the generosity of a love freely given.

It had been so long since anyone had held her, it was a joy to be caressed by a man such as this. A man who knew exactly what he wanted and knew how to get it, whilst at the same time, just by his kisses and his touch, giving her the most exquisite pleasure. Like the horses he rode so expertly, she relaxed under his weight, relying on the signals from his hands and from his body to guide her next move. Antoinetta sighed as John ran his fingers through her hair and stroked her face. From his elevated position he looked down into her green eyes and through to the very depths of her soul. He thought her wild, unbridled. The most beautiful creature he had ever beheld and he marvelled at her willingness to please him. He had tamed her. And she, too, had brought him to his knees. In the expression of their desire, they asked the other for nothing, but rather, gave of themselves. Mutually. Equally. They held each other until the crowing of the cockerels warned that dawn approached. As they lay on the blanket, still fully dressed and with their limbs entwined, the gypsy was the first to break their silence.

"I am Louella. Eet is the name my mother give me when I was a child and could not say my birth name. I am a visitor to your country and a prisoner in thees 'ouse".

John stared at her, and she felt his arms close around her protectively. She continued, *"I can not leave 'eer. I know not where I am and I 'ave no-one to 'elp me".*

44

Her English was stilted. John noted the accent but could not place it. He had met foreign ladies before in the company of Mr Rochester, but she was different somehow. Not the melodious aria of Italian, nor the relentless chatter of French, but stronger, more guttural. A voice as dusky and exciting and dark as her beauty. *"Louella"* John repeated softly, as he inhaled the scent of her hair and tenderly stroked the full length of her arm with the tips of his fingers.

"Louella, my beautiful Louella. I will help you. You need never be frightened again."

In that moment, Louella knew the existence she endured was going to change. In this man she had found, quite unexpectedly and quite against all odds, that life had new meaning.

Chapter 9

What is it that people are looking for in a relationship wondered Lisa? What do women want? Is it the same thing as men? An easy answer, and one often written about in the legion of women's glossy magazines that populate the shelves, is that men are looking for sex while women are looking for love. Lisa considered this for a while before rejecting it as being too simplistic an answer. She knew plenty of men, some of whom were friends and some of whom had been more than that, who were also looking for love, for someone to love them for who they really are. For who they really are. Those were the crucial words. To love them for who they really are, whatever and whoever that might be. But until someone works out who they are and finds someone to love them for themselves, sex seems to be an acceptable substitute. In fact, speculated Lisa, it seemed to her that many men, and many women for that matter, used sex as a substitute for spending time getting to know themselves. Far easier to drown in the arms of a lover and lose oneself in their embrace than to look in the mirror and face ourselves as we really are, particularly if we either don't recognise ourselves, or if we don't really like what we see.

What do women want? The same thing as men thought Lisa. We all want the same thing. Not the sex, although great sex is, well, great of course. What we really want is intimacy. To know and be known completely, utterly and totally, by someone else. To be known and loved by that person for who we are, not what we are. To be understood by them even if we don't always understand ourselves. To be allowed to be ourselves. No, thought Lisa, it's more than that. To be encouraged to be ourselves. To be encouraged to achieve our full potential, and for us to encourage the people we know and love to achieve theirs, safe in the knowledge that we love them and that they have our unconditional support.

True intimacy. Is all intimacy the same, wondered Lisa? Are all intimate relationships the same? No, she decided, they can't be. We are intimate with our family; with our parents and our brothers and sisters, in ways that are different to the intimacy we share with a lover. So how many kinds of intimacy are there? Lisa wasn't quite sure whether this was a psychological question or a philosophical one. Certainly the two are related. Inter-related probably. A great question for discussing in the pub, but not one that she was going to be able to answer easily here.

Lisa finally came to the conclusion that there are a number of different kinds of intimacy. The dictionary definition says that intimacy means a familiarity with something or someone. However, when we talk about being intimate with another person, it's easy to assume that we mean a sexual intimacy, but actually, thought Lisa, there are three kinds of intimacy: there's sexual intimacy of course, but there is also physical intimacy and emotional intimacy. It's no wonder that people get confused and muddle them up in their relationships.

When two people are sexually intimate with each other it's rather obvious what that means, but perhaps the other kinds of intimacy don't make so much intuitive sense. Physical intimacy is everything physical which isn't sexual. Consider a parent with their child, or a nurse with their patients. Both are good examples of situations where we are expected to touch other people, often quite intimately, but should never cross the line between a physical touch and a sexual one. Think too about the closeness of two friends, how relaxed they appear in each other's company, the ease with

47

which they interact and communicate, how they may lean against each other, or kiss each other hello and goodbye. It would be fairly easy, Lisa supposed, to see one thing and quite wrongly assume another.

Emotional intimacy is different. If sexual intimacy is developed in the horizontal position, then emotional intimacy is nurtured in the vertical one. Emotional intimacy is developed when two people talk to each other. But it's more than that thought Lisa. Emotional intimacy isn't just about talking to someone, it's about listening to them. Really listening to them. Not just learning superficial things such as whether they like broccoli or not, but learning the really important stuff. Their life story and how their many experiences have made them the person that they are today. Learning about the things they love, what they are passionate about, those things that they dislike or will avoid and even what they are afraid of.

How can you really know someone intimately if you don't talk to them and listen to them, wondered Lisa. You can physically grow up with your family and yet not know everyone's hopes and dreams. You can marry a man and bear his children yet still feel that you don't know him at all. Although these are examples of being intimate with someone, what would it be like to be truly intimate with someone in all three ways, she wondered. Lisa considered these questions amongst many others that were running through her head. She could only give answers to them for herself, not for anyone else. And although her answers might be useful for others, they could only act as a guide. Ultimately, Lisa concluded, everyone has to find their own truth and resolve the dilemma of intimacy for themselves.

Phew, thought Lisa, putting her pen down and staring out of her window over the uneven roofs of Cambridge to give her tired eyes a rest from the computer screen. All of that would have been useful to know when she was seventeen. If only someone had told her how easy it is to confuse sexual intimacy for emotional intimacy and how you can sleep with someone and think that you know them, but not really know them at all. Until she had written it all down she hadn't really realised any of it; either that it's possible, even normal, to have different kinds of intimate relationships, or that the dynamics of all romantic relationships follow the same kind of pattern over time.

What would it be like to know someone intimately in every way, she wondered, to know their innermost thoughts, their hopes and dreams. To know the things they love and those things that they would change if they could. To be intimately acquainted with the way they move and hold themselves. To know how they look when they eat and sleep. To remember their smell, their warm embrace and the feel of their lips and mouth against your own as they kiss you. To be familiar with their touch. To have heard their sighs of arousal and to know how they look at the point of ecstasy and beyond it.

Lisa imagined that it must be the most wonderful thing to feel completely connected with another person; to know them and love them to the extent that their life and their well being is as dear to you as your own. To meet a physical, intellectual and sexual partner, equal to you in every way. To experience the joyfulness of a balanced and complementary partnership, a relationship of equals. The kind of relationship that Mr Rochester eventually found with his Jane Eyre. Entangled, connected across time and space.

If true intimacy is such a wonderful thing, what's the dilemma of intimacy? Why do many people seem to try so hard to avoid it, both with themselves and with others? The paradox of intimacy is that out of fear, people avoid it, even though it's what they ultimately want. Pursuing this line of conjecture, Lisa's thoughts turned back, as they often did when she was searching for inspiration, to the writings and teachings of the classics. *"Know Thyself"*. A suggestion dating back more than three thousand years. According to her internet research it was a term ascribed to both Socrates and Plato so no-one really knows for sure who originally said it. *"Know Thyself"*. A statement originally inscribed in gold letters above the Temple of the Oracle at Delphi. *"The unexamined life is not worth living"*. What did Socrates mean by that? That self-awareness is a laudable goal? No, it means much more than that. It means that without self-reflection and the consequent self-awareness and understanding that self-examination brings, our lives are meaningless.

Lisa knew many people who would run from the opportunity to reflect on their own thoughts and behaviour. *"What's done is done, no point in dwelling on the past,"* her father would have said. Yes, but without thinking about what has been done and said, aren't we in danger of repeating past mistakes? Doesn't reflection give us the opportunity to learn something useful? thought Lisa. And what if, by thinking about what has happened to us and deciding to respond in a different way in the future, we could change that future for the better? That would be a good thing surely? Lisa could think of many occasions in her life where, had she thought about it, she could have changed the path of her life by doing or saying something differently. Times when she had been hurt or, worse, when she had inadvertently hurt someone else.

Hurts that could probably have been avoided if she had known herself better and been more self-aware.

What is it to be truly self-aware, wondered Lisa. To be truly intimate with yourself, so that you fully understand your own strengths and weaknesses, motivations, beliefs, values, emotional responses and even your own demons. What is it like to be completely comfortable with yourself and know the reasons why you do what you do? How can you love yourself if you don't know who you are? And if you don't love yourself, how can you reasonably expect anyone else to? Is it possible to be truly intimate with somebody else if you don't know yourself intimately? Lisa wasn't sure, but she doubted it somehow. On a physical and sexual level intimacy is easy. But learning about yourself, that somehow seems like a lifetime's journey, and it's clearly not one that everybody wants to take.

Lisa thought about the many people she had met in her life. Most had seemed normal, average even, whatever that means. A few, such as her grandmother, and the old man who ran the corner shop when she was a child, had seemed wise. In contrast to the experience and wisdom of age, her boyfriends had somehow seemed shallow and naïve, not yet having learned enough about themselves or the world to make them either interesting or compassionate.

So, assuming that we want to, how can we learn more about ourselves and develop the self-awareness that is a pre-requisite for emotional intimacy? Lisa didn't know. Time to go back to the library and do some more research.

Chapter 10

John and Louella met whenever fate and the comings and goings of the house allowed. Much as they could have spent a lifetime in each other's arms, John had his duties and many Estate workers relied on his instruction to busy their days. As Head Coachman, John had responsibility not just for the horses, but for those carriages, phaetons and landaus so beloved by the English gentry. They were cleaned and maintained by footmen and under-coachmen of course. But still, he had the key to the barn where they stood, waiting for their master to command them. Since the passing of old Mr Rochester, his favourite coach was rarely used, and now sat, dignified and silent, under a housekeeper's dust sheet. Magnificent in its green and gold livery, this coach was pulled by four prancing horses, matched in pace and colour. Secure against the vagaries of the English weather, it had glass windows, crushed velvet curtains and opulently padded seats and cushions. The bowed suspension springs stretched its full length making it pitch and dance on the roadway like the swaying hips of a Jamaican slave girl.

While the house and its occupants slumbered in the oblivion of darkness, for John and Louella the world awoke and the stables became their playground. In the balmy summer air, the night breeze would catch the owl on its fingertips while foxes and the wild deer danced. In such stolen moments our lovers feasted on each other; ravenous, they each devoured their time in the company of the other half of themselves. Never sated, they would talk, or walk, hand-in-hand, round the buildings and barns of John's domain, checking that all was well with the horses, that none were cast in their stables or had lathered up due to the exertions of the day.

One night, caught unexpectedly in the outside courtyard by a summer downpour, John and Louella found themselves in the coach barn. Louella stared at the rows of vehicles of which she should have been mistress. No matter. She had found her hero, a partner perfectly matched to her moods and physical desires. A man who loved her and was wholly loved by her in return. A man who could take away her fears and kiss away her pain. A man who lost himself as completely in her passionate embrace as she lost herself in his. She would not change what she had now for all the carriages in England.

Leading Louella by the hand, John lifted the housekeeper's dust sheet and opened the coach door. Taking a blanket from one of the storage boxes, he wrapped his love, first in the blanket and then in his arms, pulling her close to him so he could warm her. She lent in to him, her back pressing against his chest. John slipped his arms around her waist and let his hands glide smoothly over the silk of her dress. Cupping her covered bosom, his fingers sought a way to free her from the confines of her clothes. Gently unlacing the ribbons of the silk corset that held her in, he inhaled her scent. An exotic combination of spices and musk, as intoxicating to him as any wine. Now he kissed her delicately exposed neck and naked shoulders. An involuntary sigh escaped her lips. Twisting herself around and turning to face him, Louella deftly undid John's white cotton shirt and ran her fingers across his naked torso, bending to kiss his exposed chest as he had bent his head to kiss her breasts earlier. They made love slowly and tenderly, in ways that they knew from experience would please their partner. Passionately and deliberately, each nearly brought the other to ecstasy, then pulled back and waited for a moment to prolong the physical pleasure. Exquisite torture. Riding him astride, her skirts pushed up around her waist, Louella closed her eyes and arched her back as John used the gentle rocking of the carriage to climb still deeper into her before both exploded with the joy of mutual satisfaction. Breathless, neither could speak. Each could only gaze into the eyes and soul of the other. Tired from their passion, Louella remained sitting and rested her head on her lover's chest as he held her to him, and, finding her safe place in his arms, she slept.

••••

Not for the first time John reflected on the act of love before Louella. On the Thornfield Estate, from milk maids to farmer's wives, it was John to whom women turned, when, after a year or so of marriage, they found that they had not yet become heavy with child by their husbands. There was a subtle code amongst the women. Whispered, unspoken. It was well known that John had a knowledge of herbs and could ease minor ailments, either with his liniments and potions, or by his healing gift of touch that would massage tired muscles, or soothe an aching heart that yearned for a child.

Whatever the lady wanted. To the women on the Estate, John's services were freely given and they loved him for it. His pantry was never bare, and, should he want it, his bed was rarely empty. Because of his work with the horses and the breeding of foals on the Estate, John had an understanding

54

of women's natural rhythms and was able to tell them the best times to lay with their husbands. Of course, there were times when desperate women would lay, not just with their husband, but also with John. Inevitably, within the passing of a season they would begin to feel the flutterings and the nausea that told them for certain they were finally with child.

And then there were the society ladies. Like the women on the Estate, these were sometimes new brides, but most often they were ladies of experience with time and money and the expectation that their needs would be indulged for a certain price. These ladies were mostly wealthy widows, or those women beyond child bearing age who no longer found their husbands palatable partners. Their purpose as a vessel to provide an heir was long gone, therefore their bed was often a cold and lonely place. John didn't object. The ladies expected it and paid him well. Horizontally at least, he was more than their equal, and the service he provided was a valuable one.

The ladies would request those rooms which had the maids' entrance on the internal house corridor close to the servants' staircase. Because of his travels with Mr Rochester, John knew the back stairs and secret passageways of most of the finer country houses of England. As a rich and handsome bachelor, Edward Fairfax Rochester was in great demand by all of the mothers who had a daughter in need of a husband and an eye to his considerable fortune. Blanche Ingram had such a mother.

Servants were not allowed to use the main doorways to the salons or bedrooms of the house. They were expected to be invisible, using the hidden servants' doors secreted in the wooden panelling or wallpaper of the walls. Each ingress was difficult to see. An invisible door for invisible servants. They would slip in and out by way of the servants' corridor, a busy internal runway intended to mimic the design of the main house. Built on the inside as an echo to the outside structure. When the room was empty, a maid or manservant would enter with water, towels or flowers, leaving the door slightly ajar, slipping out again quickly and quietly as if they were never there. Only at night would certain invited servants be welcome to linger and stay a while.

John was no fool. He knew that if his services were unavailable or if he chose not to oblige the ladies, there would always be a manservant or an under-butler to provide whatever amusement the lady in question desired. John had been in demand from the age of seventeen, when, as a strapping young stable boy he had first come to the attention of the Duchess of X...shire and her party. Like the horses they rode hard to hounds during the day, by night he was a tool to be used for their convenience and pleasure. They taught him how to satisfy a woman, and they had taught him well.

But they had not taught him how to love. If lust is the stirrings of physical desire without the attendant emotions, then passion is the place where physical desire and emotion meet. Only with Louella, and for the first time in his life, John now experienced the heady combination of true passion. Of lust and love; intoxicating and addictive. Moments in time that even as they occurred, seemed unreal. High on passion and emotion, they made love in the hours between sleeping and waking when the rest of the house and its Estate were asleep. Intimate strangers, they slowly learned each other's life stories, hopes and dreams. As John held Louella in his arms and watched her sleeping, a faint smile of satisfaction still on her lips, he knew that he would willingly rescue her. Yes, he would take her home to the warm winds, sandy beaches and blue skies she spoke of, where the sweet scent of flowers hung in the air. There was nothing to keep him here. His arms and his bed would be empty without her. Without her, his life would have no meaning. He would find a way to release her from the prison that held her and she would save him from a life without the passion of love. As he watched her sleep, he began to plan their escape.

Chapter 11

"1 missed call".

There was a text message on Lisa's mobile from Caroline Harvey, the editor of *Psychologies Magazine*.

"Article commission for July. Call me".

Fantastic, thought Lisa, I wonder what she has in mind. This was the exciting bit, and the scary bit actually. Lisa loved writing, especially the stimulation of a new idea. Piecing together fragmented psychological research like a brain-teasing puzzle, weaving the different strands of information together to make a cohesive and easily readable article that was useful to people. It was a great job to have. But until a piece of writing was finished she was always scared that she couldn't do it, that she would get writer's block or wouldn't write as well as she knew she could. She dialled Caroline's number.

"Hi Caroline, it's Lisa. Thanks for your call, what do you have in mind?"

Ten minutes later, Lisa was on her way to the library, half formed ideas swirling around in her head and colliding with each other in the way that creative thoughts often did. Caroline had asked for an article about sex. About the different kinds of sex that we may encounter on our journey through life. Caroline wanted the article to explain not only the different kinds of sex, but also how sex can be many things, and how, within a relationship, we can often confuse one type of sex for another, so that the lines between them become blurred. How we may sometimes use sex almost like a drug to help us change our physical and emotional states, and how recognising the different kinds of sex that exist can help to give us more control over the kinds of sex that we choose to have.

Two days later Lisa was frustrated. Not because she had spent two whole days researching about sex, which had just reminded her that she wasn't having sex of any sort, but for two other, quite different reasons. Firstly, she couldn't find the kind of information she was looking for within existing psychological research, and secondly, after talking to a number of friends of both sexes, she found that no-one could agree and she was more confused than ever.

The boys were the worst. They just joked around and said that all kinds of sex were good. Kinky sex, outdoor sex, tied-up sex, dressing up sex and especially party sex. They were happy to have any and all types of sex, and as far as Lisa could tell, just about anytime and anywhere. Not particularly helpful, thought Lisa, she was writing for *Psychologies Magazine*, not *Playboy*! She did find a couple of rather bad jokes on the internet which had made her laugh, but ultimately, they didn't help much either: Two men were talking in a bar. One says that he's having Social Security sex. *"What's that?"* asks the other man. *"I get a little bit every month, but it's not enough to live on,"* replied the first. The second man says that he likes Smurf sex best. *"What's that?"* asks the first. *"It's the kind of sex you have on your honeymoon. You just keep doing it until you're blue in the face."* The second joke was even worse and definitely not repeatable in polite company.

Her girlfriends were slightly more helpful, although Kate had simplified things a little too much perhaps. Like the boys, Kate also thought that there were only two types of sex: good sex and bad sex. She went on to say that although she'd rather have good sex any day of the week, twice a day if it was really good, she thought that good chocolate was better than bad sex which was why she had put on five pounds recently. Lisa had laughed and was tempted to agree; however it didn't exactly help her to write the article.

After another week of thinking about sex for most of the time and with the deadline looming, Lisa decided that she would have to try another approach. Rather than continuing to research a subject about which surprisingly little seemed to have been written, she would look back over her own relationships and write from her own perspective, then test out her theories. She could bounce ideas off her friends, some of whom it had to be said, had considerably more experience than she did, 'in the bedroom department'. She giggled at herself, that was a phrase her mother would have used, and she knew, both from her research and her own memory, that although some sex obviously did happen in the bedroom, lots of sex happened in other places as well.

Lisa spent the next few days looking back over past relationships, both hers and those of her friends and family. She considered numerous conversations, and eventually drew up a list of all the different kinds of sex that she could think of. It was a very long list and she was faintly amused to notice that she'd only 'done' about a third of them. Something that she hoped to change if she ever met the right man, whatever the 'right man' was. She briefly wondered whether she should stop waiting for Mr Right and settle for Mr Right Now, but she knew that her beliefs and values wouldn't allow her to do that. She would rather be single and celibate than spend intimate time with a man she did not love and who did not love her equally in return.

In order to find some kind of clarity regarding the list, Lisa knew that she would need to simplify it. After more thought and many more jottings, she came to the eventual decision that there are six different categories of sex and everything on her list would fit into at least one of them.

The first kind of sex is Loving sex and, she thought, was the romantic ideal she had grown up with. The motivation behind Loving sex is, as you would expect, love. Therefore when someone 'makes love' with a partner, the driving force behind it is emotional in nature rather than just a physical, 'making out'. The second kind of sex, in contrast to the first, is Passionate sex. Rather obviously, this is where lust fits in. Passionate sex is driven by physical desire, and might or might not also involve love. Third on the list was Recreational sex. This was where Lisa had included sex between friends, party sex, kinky sex, swinging, dogging, voyeurism, dressing up sex, legal pornography and all of those other kinds of sex that were driven by the desire to have fun and a good time rather than anything else.

Functional sex came next. Slightly more difficult to explain, this kind of sexual activity includes all of those encounters not driven by emotional or physical desire or the impetus of amusing oneself for a while. Where you 'do it mechanically' for the sake of a partner when you don't really want to, when it's duty or because someone is paying you for your services, and sex becomes 'just a job' or a task on a tick list to complete. Not the kind of sex Lisa would want, although there had been times at the very end of a dying relationship where, in its death throws, the sex had felt functional rather than Loving, Passionate or Recreational and she had been relieved when the relationship had finally ended. Sighing inwardly at the memories, but happy that she wasn't in that position any longer, Lisa turned back to her list.

The next category was rather beautiful she thought. Healing sex is designed to put someone back together and make them whole again after they have been hurt in some way. The hurt is most often emotional, although it may also have had its roots in sexual or physical pain. Healing sex only happens with a compassionate and generous lover. Its purpose is to comfort and nurture and will often be gentle, tender and loving, although Passionate sex can also be profoundly healing depending on what someone might need. Healing sex was much, much better than chocolate, thought Lisa, even good chocolate.

The last category on her list was the kind of sex that Lisa would rather not think about, but unfortunately is the kind that is all too familiar for many people. Destructive sex is the opposite of Healing sex. Its purpose is to manipulate and control, and is often more about power or punishment than the sexual act itself. Incest and rape are examples of Destructive sex, as is a relationship where one partner either gives or withholds sex as a punishment or a reward. There's nothing loving or generous about that scenario thought Lisa, despite the ways in which some people try to justify their behaviour. It's just sick sex and Lisa wanted no part of it. She felt that it was important to include it on the list though, otherwise there would be a category missing. Recognising something and being able to name it gives people their power back, and once you can recognise Destructive sex for what it is, you can take steps to avoid it and choose to have one of the other, more healthy kinds of sexual relationship instead.

Amongst Lisa's girlfriends, Susan had said something interesting. She remarked that the kind of sex people have is often a reflection of the dynamics of the relationship that they are involved in. This suggests that you are likely to have Loving sex within a loving relationship, Passionate sex within a passionate one, and Destructive sex within a sick relationship. This isn't definitive of course. People and relationships are infinitely complex. Likewise, the lines between the different kinds of sex are not precise and at best have blurred edges.

Playing around with this idea took Lisa's thoughts off in all sorts of directions in order to explore the possibilities of what Susan had suggested. In theory, because the dynamics of a relationship are constantly changing over time, like the shifting sand banks of a delta, all kinds of sex are possible within a relationship. Recreational sex can become Passionate sex or sometimes morph into Loving sex if you happen to fall in love with someone whilst having a good time with them. Healing sex, because it is caring and generous, can become Loving sex just as Loving sex can sometimes be deeply Healing. Passionate sex can become Destructive if the dynamics of the relationship become dangerously distorted, and even previously Loving sex can become Functional over time if the quality of the loving relationship changes.

Lisa considered the idea that people could have certain preferences for the kind of sex they engage in at different times of their lives. For example, Passionate, Stage One sex can be highly addictive, and can keep people constantly stuck in Stage One relationships. Healing sex might be what people need after they have experienced a bereavement or a loss such as divorce. Lisa knew many guys who had enjoyed playing the field for years but had happily exchanged Recreational, party sex for Loving sex when they had found the right girl to settle down with. She also knew a few girlfriends who had gleefully exchanged Functional sex with their husbands for Recreational party sex on the swinging scene. For some, it had given them a new lease of life. For others, it had meant the end of their marriage.

It occurred to Lisa that two people could be intimately involved with each other and, without being aware of it, they could each be having a different kind of sex. Lisa had once made the mistake of having a brief relationship with someone whom she thought had feelings for her. She had confused passion with love. Loving someone makes you vulnerable to being hurt and she had wrongly assumed that he felt the same way as she did. When she finally learned the truth, that he had been having Recreational sex and she had been just a plaything, she felt like a fool. She still thought about him occasionally, he had been a hard act to follow. But that's the nature of loss. Memories going around in circles, and all the emotions associated with those memories swirling around with them until you can finally let them go.

Lisa was getting tired and her mind had started to wander. She was cross with herself for allowing her thoughts to drift back to that particular man and that particular relationship. She wanted to look forwards not backwards, but memories of him kept catching her unawares and hooking her back in time. Tidying up the scribbled writings that lay on the desk, she had a quick look at the diary to remind herself of her schedule for the next day. After all, she still had her studies to attend to. The article wasn't quite finished, but she had enough of its structure to talk it through with some friends over the next few days and then tie up its loose ends into a neat bow ready for Caroline's deadline. Writing it had given her some ideas for future articles, which was good because the freelance fee was a generous one and she had some new books to pay for.

Chapter 12

Some time had passed since Louella had been able to spend time with John. Time that felt like an eternity.

Midnight saw her hurrying along the path to Coachman's Cottage, her stomach knotted with anxiety. They had made no arrangement. What if John wasn't there? Where could he be? They had stopped meeting in the hay loft above the stables some time ago and now his little cottage, bathed in moonlight, was as familiar to Louella as her own rooms on the third floor. At the gate, Louella slid into the overgrown garden and made her way up the path, trying not to tread on the snails that meandered their silver trails across it. She let herself in through the back entrance and locked the door behind her with the key that hung on the hook beside it. The cottage was still and dark. Tentatively, her heart thumping inside her chest, and painfully conscious of every breath, she slipped silently up the narrow wooden stairs in the centre of the house to John's bedroom where the door stood ajar, beckoning her. There was a shape in the bed; a blanket-covered hump that matched her lover's form and height, exactly where it should be. Her relief was palpable. How could she have doubted him?

Her trembling fingers could not undo the buttons of her dress. Yet, nor could she sleep in it. She must wait a while, either until she was calmed, or until her lover awoke. Sometimes, when he was watching her, she disrobed in front of him, stripping slowly and sensuously as her mother had taught her would arouse a man's passions, allowing the moonlight that streamed through the cottage windows to dance on her soft, oiled, exotic olive skin. It was a ritual that thrilled her as much as it did her lover. John loved to watch her, and she adored being watched. At other times she disrobed downstairs, arriving in his chamber naked, a willing slave slipping silently into the warmth of his bed and the warmth of his embrace. Tonight, Louella examined her sleeping lover's face, regarding him adoringly before waking him with the soft kiss on his lips that in his dreams he had long waited for.

By the time their lover's kiss ended some minutes later, she knew that he was ready and impatient for more. It was obvious that John did not want to wait to feel her body beneath his. So she made him wait, teasing him exquisitely with her fingers and her mouth and prolonging his interest by making him slowly undress her, one button and one ribbon at a time ...

As all lovers know, the time they spend in their beloved's arms passes all too soon and no amount of time can ever be enough. So it was for Louella and John. They both knew that with dawn's early light at approximately thirty minutes past the hour of four, the slumbering household would begin to rouse itself and would be a hive of activity an hour later. Louella was in no hurry to leave John's warm embrace, but she knew that should Grace Poole wake and find her gone, her punishment would be severe.

Superstition enforced a strict code of always leaving an abode via the same door one had entered it by. To which end, Louella turned the key in the door before leaning her weight against John's chest as he wrapped his arms around her, warming her back against his naked chest as he wrapped her in his arms and kissed the nape of her elegant neck once more before parting. She opened the door and stepped out over the threshold into the still, chill air of morning. The flurry of bustling material caught her eye. In the distance, not quite a hundred yards away, the figure of a woman fled the cottage at a trot, heading back towards the Hall in the early morning light. But who would be here on the path at this hour? After all, the path only led from the stables out to the Estate fields passing John's solitary cottage on the way. Apart from visiting Coachman's Cottage, there was no reason for anyone to come down the path at all. Surprised and immediately both suspicious and concerned in equal measure, Louella turned in the doorway to look back at John.

As she did so, her foot touched against a letter, obviously hand-delivered and left for John leaning against his door. Immediately suspicious, Louella bent down and picked the missive up, deftly opening the sealed flap with her delicate, nimble fingers. After all, there could be no secrets between them, could there?

"Meet me by the kitchen door after breakfast".

Louella gasped. Her worst fears realised in that instant; her hopes and dreams shattered into a million shards. John's sweet words of affection and proclamations of love had been false after all. Oh, she had been a fool to trust him, an idiot to believe that he would want her for anything more than his gypsy whore. With that thought in her head, and with hurt and fury welling up inside her, she turned on her lover.

"Wot 'ees thees? You peeg, you filthy peeg. I 'ate you, I weesh I 'ad neever set eyes on you. Go to your filthee lover after breekfast. I neever wont to see you ageen."

With the words of the note still swimming in her head and with tears stinging in her eyes, Louella fled the sanctuary of John's cottage and ran back to the Hall and her prison. Now incarcerated by her own choosing, to avoid a chance meeting in the Hall's gardens or the Estate fields with the man who had ripped her heart from her chest and destroyed all hopes and dreams of any kind of happiness in her future, Louella remained indoors for weeks, sobbing and desolate, alone, lonely and inconsolable. She was now tormented and made miserable, not by her husband, but by the unbidden thoughts of her lover with another woman.

Repeatedly revisiting every minute of their relationship in her mind, Louella ignored the gossip and stories that Grace Poole brought up from the kitchen along with her supper. Although she missed John more than she had thought possible and longed for him to touch her once more, to hold her and tell her that all would be well as he covered her mouth and neck in tender kisses, she simply could not capitulate and leave the confinement of her room to visit him. She had, after all, ended their union with harsh and spiteful words. She knew she had damaged their relationship fundamentally and felt in her heart that he would not want to see her any more than he could forgive her. She could not forgive herself, so how could she expect charity from him?

She did have one visitor however. One night, some time after midnight when sleep was welcoming her into its warm embrace, she thought she heard the heavy tread of male footsteps in the corridor entering her chambers. She awoke, startled, to a face leaning over her, a face distorted and grotesque, ruddy and bloated by an excess of port. A hand grabbed her wrist in a vice-like grip and she found herself being dragged from her bed.

"You dirty whore, I wish you were dead. I rue the day I ever set eyes on you. You bewitched me against my will with your black magic charms all those years ago. But now I will have me a new wife, a slip of a girl so pure and so innocent I will love her for all eternity. If I were more of a man, I would kill you now with my bare hands and be rid of you forever. No, Bertha, you will not thwart me, I will have her."

As the attacker dragged her across the room and threw her roughly to the floor, Louella knocked her hip against the wooden chest in the fall. The pain made her cry out in anguish. She instinctively covered her face in case he struck her as he had done so often in the past. But, despite shielding herself against the heat of his anger, she couldn't help but look up into the wild eyes of her husband.

Chapter 13

"Pay particular attention to endings, because their hues will forever colour your memories of the relationship and your willingness to re-enter it". Dr. Martin Seligman, author of Authentic Happiness and past President of the American Psychological Association.

The beginnings and endings of relationships were themes that Lisa was particularly interested in. She found the psychology of relationships endlessly fascinating and, of course, all relationships, every one of every kind of relationship, whether it is a friendship, a relationship with a new boss, a colleague or, more excitingly, with a lover, all start with a beginning and conclude their lifecycle with an eventual end.

She wasn't quite sure what had brought about this unusual interest, except that she always seemed to be able to remember exactly how she had met someone, and the nature of their parting the last time that she had seen or spoken with them. Sometimes this was in excruciating detail, especially if their parting had been painful or embarrassing in some way. With the notable exception of Martin Seligman's quote on the subject, the endings of relationships weren't something that she had ever read anything about; perhaps it would be useful to give them more thought and explore them more deeply.

Thinking about how Louella had first encountered John, it was easy to imagine the scene from his perspective; a beautiful and exotic gypsy girl sitting astride a black stallion, appearing in his life as if out of nowhere and disappearing back into dawn's early light like a spectre in a dream. He had not known from whence she came or, afterwards, if he would ever see her again. She was a stranger on the Estate and that only added to her mystery. However, the same story from her ancestor's perspective had been a very different one. It was true enough that she hadn't actually physically met the tall, good-looking coachman until that night, but in her mind she had known him for ten years; watched him grow from a boy into a man through her windows, and imagined every scene of their lives together. For Louella, meeting John had been the fulfilment of her imagination, an opportunity to finally live her dream and be touched by the man she had already made her hero. Fantasy made flesh. A dangerous game.

Beginnings. Sometimes it is only possible to know in retrospect that a beginning is going to be significant. Easy then to overlook it at the time, to sneeze when one should be breathing deeply and inhaling the aroma of the years to come. For Lisa, a previous lover called Mark had been such a scent. Periodically she had caught a whiff of the smell of him on the winds of time, long after their relationship had turned from the initial storm that had disquieted her, lifting her off her feet and temporarily destabilising her, into the Santa Ana of the warm wind of a friendship that had comforted her over the years, and in truth, continued to do so now, even though they were geographically and emotionally miles apart.

Beginnings occur in many ways, but whichever way one meets a new friend, a colleague, a lover or even a soul mate, a universal truth is that, just as every relationship must have a starting point, so too must it eventually have an end. Both of these temporal events are important in terms of the influence that they have on how we remember someone and our memories of the times that we spent with them. However, an ending is not always as easy to define as a beginning; endings are not always so clear cut and obvious.

Sometimes what may appear to be an ending isn't one at all, it's just a gap on the winding path of a friendship that gets picked up again later along our life's journey. Neither had Lisa thought about the colours of endings before, although the idea made sense, from the cool blue hues of a friendship that gradually drifts apart to the red forks of a heated argument and an angry separation.

That the way a relationship ends will affect our desire to re-enter that relationship, assuming we have the opportunity to do so, wasn't something that Lisa had ever really thought about before. Once, working as an intern in a particularly progressive and forward thinking organisation, before she had taken her first degree, she experienced an exit interview before leaving to join another company. She remembered that it had been a voluntary conversation and the interviewer was a junior psychologist from the human resources department. Together they discussed the reasons why she had chosen to leave, how she felt about the organisation, what she would change, or do differently, if she was one of the senior managers, and whether she had any suggestions regarding how the employees' working conditions could be improved. Lisa had been impressed. The psychologist told her that in her experience, most people either left managers whom they didn't like for one reason or another, or they left in order to find better pay and working conditions. This organisation had wanted to retain its talented staff where it could and certainly wanted to avoid any management malpractice. Lisa had warmed to the psychologist and although she had indeed left for a better position, she still remembered the company fondly. It had an inclusive and relaxed atmosphere that she had enjoyed and she often recommended it to people. She would happily work for them again if an appropriate opportunity presented itself.

However, Lisa also remembered the pleadings and angry rants of a boyfriend she had parted from because of his drinking. Even thinking about him now made her shudder. She had refused entreaties from him to reconnect on Facebook and Bebo; there was no way she would consider, not even for a second, picking up the reins of that particular relationship. In fact, they were not reins, they were entrails; an ill-conceived friendship that was definitely better off dead.

Musing on the endings of relationships made Lisa reflect on what psychology can tell us about loss and the emotions we experience as a result of it. Today, with divorce more common, we are much more familiar with relationships that end. Some relationships finish suddenly, others atrophy and die slowly, over time. But the experience of grief and the process that we go through when we have lost someone or something is not limited only to marriage. Feelings of loss occur within us relating to more than simply people. We can mourn the loss of innocence, the loss of a job, an adored pet, a friendship, or of some other relationship, just as we will grieve for the physical death of a loved one.

In fact, some psychologists suggest that it is harder to recover from divorce, the death of a marriage, than it is to recover from the death of a loved one. This may sound rather strange, until you consider that when someone divorces you, they have rejected and chosen to leave you. Whereas, in the case of bereavement, one has to assume that the person we have lost did not choose to die.

Chapter 14

After her husband's attack, his abject loathing of her now more evident than ever, in his thoughts he compared his first wife to the woman he would make his second. If it were possible, Louella now felt even more alone. Having lost in totality everything she held dear, all that gave life meaning, she now had nothing left to live for. Much to her amazement and thoroughly miserable as she still was, this realisation led to a sense of freedom. Not caring whether one lives or dies creates a new kind of recklessness to which Louella was far from immune.

Many had been the times when Louella hated her husband quite as much as he detested her. Now she had nothing to lose, and whilst the bruises on her arms and legs were still blue-black, an idea crept into her mind. She would carry out his own threat against her and kill him in his bed as he slept. She liked the idea of fire's serpent tongues licking at her husband before consuming him whole; swallowing him as the python its prey. The house would blaze around them, killing her tormentor and taking her to a final rest. She had no thoughts of the servants or any house guests; they could take their chances and escape if they could. They cared not for her misery, and she gave no thought to them. They were bit-part players in the fantasy of her reality; not real to her, nor she to them.

As Grace Poole slept in the early hours, Louella donned the maid's uniform once again and taking a candle from her bedside table, slipped out of her rooms and down the narrow wooden servants' stairs to the second floor where she knew her husband would be sleeping. She entered his chamber through the hidden servants' entrance, made invisible as a door in the dark oak wood panelling and stood in her husband's lair. The fire in the grate offered flickering amber light by which she could see a form, lying flat and still in a four poster bed similar in design to her own.

Having rehearsed the scene in her mind many times over, Louella wasted no time in swiftly crossing the floor to look at her estranged husband's comatose face one last time, before bending down to light the two tapestry curtains at the foot of the bed. As she watched the flames begin to lick upwards towards the ceiling, she let out a delighted laugh; soon she would be rid of him. With that, she fled her erstwhile Master's chambers, returning to her own rooms above him, climbing into bed and closing her eyes to await the blessed embrace of flames and the darkness of death.

• • • •

For those of you who are familiar with the story of *Jane Eyre*, you will know that, on this occasion at least, Louella's clumsy attempt at arson was unsuccessful and Jane saved Mr Rochester from the fire. An act that brought them closer together and proved to be one of the pivotal points in their relationship. However, predictably, Louella's actions carried with them certain consequences; consequences that will become evident shortly.

• • • •

Once roused from his bed by Jane Eyre and having doused the flames that threatened to engulf him, Edward Fairfax Rochester pulled his new love to his chest and embraced her so tightly that she feared he might crush her. He then sent Jane to her room, instructing her to lock the door securely behind her. A rather futile command as, should Louella have wished to enter Jane's bedchamber, she would simply have entered it via the servants' door in the wooden panelling that formed an invisible part of the chamber's wall. However, his close brush with death had alerted Mr Rochester to certain information that he hadn't considered before; namely, that there were times when his first wife was evidently free to roam the corridors of the Hall as she wished, and secondly, that she knew where he slept. Actions must be taken to ensure the safety of all members of his household, and he must take those actions forthwith.

In the long days of isolation that followed Louella's attack on her husband, she was not alone in the torment of her grief and its attendant emotions of utter desolation and despair. She could think of nothing but John and every thought wounded her in ways more painful than she could ever have imagined. It had now been six weeks since John had last seen Louella in his cottage doorway when accusations were made and harsh words spoken. In the first few weeks of their separation, John's anger and pride had driven any grief from his heart. But now, after so long, he, too, was tormented by the strength of his feelings for Louella and he felt her loss keenly. It was impossible to stay away any longer. With the Master in the house, John knew he was taking a terrible risk, but he would rather have died a thousand deaths than wait even one more night to see the woman he wanted more than anything or anyone he had ever known. He resolved to see his beautiful gypsy that night, whatever the cost.

As the stable clock struck ten, John slipped into the Hall via one of the many side entrances and strode purposefully deeper into the house where he found the maze of servants' corridors that took him invisibly upwards towards the third floor. Upon reaching the locked door behind which his love was imprisoned, he took out of his trouser pocket a folded piece of rather dirty cream waxed canvas. Used for saddlery repairs, it was stiff enough to slip under the door, through the gap which allowed the wooden floors and doors of the Hall to shift with the seasons as the house swelled and then shrank again, moving imperceptibly over time. Taking the narrow metal race from where he had stored it down his gaiters, he poked the rod through the door lock, so the key was pushed out and fell down onto the canvas below. Carefully, he took the canvas in his fingers and gently pulled the grubby cloth towards himself. The canvas slid smoothly under the door with his prize resting on it. Turning the key in the lock, his insides twisted in unison with the iron in his hand. Folding and replacing the canvas in his pocket, slowly and silently he let himself in, placing the key back in the lock behind him.

Flickering candlelight beckoned him down a narrow corridor. He heard a muffled whimpering that reminded him of a puppy the first night it was separated from its mother. Entering the room he was prepared to come face to face with Grace Poole, but not prepared for the sight that confronted him. Louella in her nightclothes; her long white dress of embroidered cotton scrunched up around her, huddled, sobbing and dirty on the wooden floor. His barefoot princess tiny and helpless, tethered to the wall like an animal, by a thin chain secured tightly around her wrist, the padlock digging deep into her bruised arm.

Wrapped in a coarse woollen blanket and snoring loudly in the rocking chair by the window, slept her warden, obviously the worse for wear having guzzled too much gin. Surprised by her visitor, Louella gasped in sharp recognition, but turned to the wall to hide her face from him, tears wet on her cheeks. He saw how the chain bit into her, and saw, despite her partially covered face, a bruised blue-green eye and red swollen cheek.

Seeing Louella in such wretched misery, in an instant he forgave her everything. His love for her so hot it could have rivalled the sun, his rage so cold, had it been manifest it would have blackened the May blossom tips as quickly as a late hoar frost. He strode towards her and dropped to his knees, gently lifting her hair from her tear-stained face. Still she looked away.

"Oh Louella. Louella my love. Forgive me, I knew not the torture he puts you through."

"John, you 'ave come for me. But you must not stay, eet ees not safe. Ee will come."

"I care not. Let me face him. I will rip his heart out."

Her hero had come for her, to rescue her and save her from this torture. Louella knew now, by the look of tenderness in his eyes, that John wanted her. Any foolish pride she had once felt had long since gone, she wanted only to be held in his arms and to feel his soft lips wipe away her tears with his kisses. Louella sobbed in John's arms and clung to him for some time, before he gently pushed her away and looked at her.

"Where is the key for this infernal padlock my love?"

"Eet ees wiv 'er, she 'as it 'wiv 'er kays on 'er kay ring. Be carefool my love."

"Will she wake?"

"No, I fink not, she 'as been drinkin' 'er gin. She will not wake 'til dawn breaks."

John raised himself and walked over to Grace Poole's sleeping form, carefully lifting the keys from the end of the chain tucked into her apron pocket. He unlocked the metal tether that tied his lover to the wall, putting it to one side, determined to remove it when he left. Lifting Louella from the floor, he carried her to the bed and laid her gently on the blankets that covered it. Next, he tended to the fading embers of the fire, adding logs and coal to warm the room. Aware that Mr Rochester could enter the room at any moment, but caring little for that, he bent down, removing his rough leather gaiters and his boots before climbing up onto the high mattress of Louella's oak four poster bed. Sitting next to her, he swept her up in his arms once again, positioning her so he could cradle her and hold her to him as a loving parent would hold and rock a sick child. Louella bent her knees around John's body as she sat on his lap and snuggled into his masculine chest, breathing in the smell of him and of the horses on his clothes. He kissed the top of her head as he pulled her to him, and kept a watchful eye on both Grace Poole and the corridor. As his lover's sobs slowly subsided and her breathing became deeper, finally, she slept.

Chapter 15

Quite a lot is written about grief and the process of bereavement. However, very little is written regarding the loss of a romantic relationship and how to cope with those emotions we feel as a result of its ending. There seems to be an unspoken code of stoicism, after all, *"There are plenty more fish in the sea"*. Those words were her mother's, thought Lisa. She could hear her saying them right now; see her standing by the sink with a dishcloth in her hand as she bent over the remains of supper. That was fine if you wanted to date a guppy, but Lisa had never thought it a particularly helpful comment. Her mother was quite right in the sense of there being many people in the world whom we could fall in love with, but in the West, particularly with regard to romantic love, there remains an enduring myth of 'The One'. Every girl wants to find her Prince Charming, and every boy wants to find his own special Princess to awaken with the magic of his kiss.

But what happens when it ends, wondered Lisa, what happens when all our dreams and hopes for the future with a special person die? Regardless of the way that a romantic relationship ends, the cold, hard and often painful reality is that our lover is gone and we must continue our lives without them however much it might hurt; and sometimes it gnaws away at us and hurts so much as to be almost unbearable. Although the process of grief is similar for everyone, Lisa knew, both from her studies and from watching her friends, that each of us varies in the way that we deal with the loss of a relationship.

Jane Eyre, after a short period of time when she didn't care whether she lived or died, had chosen to recreate her life within the warmth of the family who had rescued her from the inhospitable moors. To ensure that she could not be found, Jane changed her name, and once she had regained her strength, with the assistance of St. John Rivers, found employment as the schoolmistress of a small country school for local girls, and, although she thought of Mr Rochester often, she recreated a life for herself without him. In contrast to Jane, Edward Fairfax Rochester felt that his life had ended the day that Jane had left him; living a half-life and becoming reclusive even before the tragedy that had taken both the Hall and his sight from him.

Most writing on the subject seems to assume that grief after loss is a linear process that people have to work through one step and one stage at a time. But this assumption does a disservice to anyone who has experienced the ending of a relationship and has struggled to cope with it. Lisa knew how raw grief could feel. How, just when you felt that things were finally getting easier, memories and thoughts could surface that knock you sideways, like a rogue wave stealing your feet out from underneath you in the surf, leaving you sprawling on the ground and struggling for breath. Easy to be swept out to sea if you weren't careful.

Recovering from loss is a circular journey rather than a straight line; a meandering pathway and an uphill climb, strewn with rocks and boulders and slippery shingle that can make us lose our footing at any time. Sadness sometimes makes us step back on our journey to recovery, sometimes makes us tumble and fall, metaphorically grazing our hands and knees in the process, and giving us yet more emotional wounds and bruises that need their own time to heal.

Grief after loss is normal. It's a natural and human response. Despite the pain of it, grieving allows us to remember just what it was that we valued about the relationship and what it is that we will miss. Remembering those things and paying attention to them, even if it's uncomfortable at the time, allows us the joy of recognition when we find elements of them again in the future.

In our human experience of loss, the first stage is usually shock. Even if the end of a relationship was expected, and even if we ourselves chose to end it, we can sometimes be momentarily thrown off balance by the punctuation mark of a full stop. There are exceptions of course. In an abusive relationship the first response may well be one of relief, but what's described here is the ending of a normal romantic attachment, if such a thing exists. It's also important to remember that the stages are not in any way linear; like the flight of a butterfly the elements of the stages meander and circle, alight, linger and take flight again, all in a seemingly random and chaotic pattern.

Shock, or its milder cousin, surprise, is often either accompanied, or closely followed by, denial, where we imagine that the ending hasn't really occurred; that it's all a horrible dream, from which we will soon awake, or that the object of our affections will come to their senses and return forthwith to our arms. At this stage we can also be confused and fearful of the future. Our confusion and sadness is sometimes replaced by anger, when we lash out, paradoxically hurting ourselves and others in the process of trying to make ourselves feel better. We might desperately try to renegotiate the relationship, bargaining and making promises that may be difficult or even impossible to keep.

Accompanied by feelings of helplessness and despair, if we are not able to rescue a relationship, our bargaining may give way to depression when we realise that our lover is lost to us. This stage can last for what seems like forever as we lose interest in everything and everyone around us. A reconciliation, if unsuccessful, will only serve to send us spiralling back in time to an earlier stage of the grief process as our emotions loop around; such is the roller coaster ride of the feelings of loss. Eventually, usually, our emotions stabilise and our feelings of grief become less raw. We detach ourselves from thoughts of a future with our ex-beloved and begin to accept that there are, indeed, 'plenty more fish in the sea'.

Often, it isn't so much the loss of someone that's so difficult to cope with, but our own feelings of rejection that, having once been chosen as special, we are no longer wanted, no longer a pre-requisite for the happiness of a person we had once considered to be extraordinary.

Of course, it could be argued that the best way to recover from the loss of a relationship is to begin a new one; to find someone else and experience the giddy heights that intimacy with another person often brings. However, much as this sentiment may be true in its own way, to begin a new relationship too early, before we are ready to move on, short-circuits our opportunity to grow. An opportunity to learn more about ourselves and others, and to learn those life lessons that in some mysterious way are meant to make us better friends and better people. To make us somehow more considerate, kinder, more sensitive and understanding, more tolerant of our own and others' frailties, and, greater perhaps than anything else, to make us more forgiving.

Having learnt what we can from our experience, uncomfortable or painful as it may have been, helps us to finally accept our loss and the situation we now find ourselves in. Only when we can take the learning and let the emotions go can we ultimately recover our balance and get on with our lives. But before we can do that, very often we also need to review and reassess our lives, exploring our options and making new plans for the future.

However, there are some people who never recover from the loss of a relationship. Although it is quite rare, and may also depend on certain personality traits such as high levels of neuroticism, or a need for control, occasionally people integrate loss into the very fabric of their sense of identity, thereby making it impossible for them to move forward. Miss Havisham is an extreme literary example of this. In *Great Expectations* we know her as a man-hating, bitter and twisted spinster, forever wearing the faded wedding dress in which she was jilted at the altar. She became rooted in anger, stuck for all time and unable to form a healthy romantic attachment with anyone else. Needless to say, she damaged the relationships of the people closest to her and she did not meet a good end.

Painful as it is to think about, ultimately, loss gives us the opportunity to review and reassess our lives, to learn new lessons and develop greater understanding and a more compassionate side to ourselves. Of course, no-one in the throws of passion or the agony of a lost love is remotely interested in such an existentialist position. Even Jane Eyre would have agreed that philosophical debate is meaningless when your heart is breaking.

Chapter 16

Upon waking the next morning, Grace Poole assumed the Master had made a visit in the night and removed the chain that bound Louella to the house. Ashamed at being found in a drunken stupor and afraid, too, for the security of her position, she mentioned the night's events to no-one, but went about her business as if all was as it should be. There was a subtle change in her attitude, however, as she evidently thought it prudent to take a little more care of her charge. As the Master had obviously softened his grip on his wife, she, too, now softened slightly in her ways. Although she would still steal Louella's trinkets when the opportunity arose, she no longer laced Louella's food with opiates or forced her to drink brandy to subdue her.

Then something happened which was to change the course of the future for all of them. Thornfield Hall was full and all of a fluster. The Ingram party was expected tomorrow and for the past two weeks Mrs Fairfax, the housekeeper, had organised a small army to scrub and clean, wash, darn and polish the whole house until the Hall shone like a new pin. Nor had the stables escaped the deliberations of brushes, brooms and cloths. Every horse and every carriage now also stood gleaming to attention waiting for the excitement and gossip that only a large party of ladies and gentlemen will bring. The words whispered on servants' stairwells and in the kitchen at suppertime were, *"romance, beauty, love"* and *"marriage"*.

Even from the third floor, Louella also felt the animated anticipation of the household as she watched the many preparations from her windows. It sometimes seemed as if a hundred deliveries a day arrived at the tradesman's door by the kitchens. She watched too for glimpses of John but rarely saw him. Grace Poole seemed more attentive than usual and so slipping away was difficult. Louella could only hope that the excitement of the party might afford some means of escape, albeit temporarily.

On the morning the Ingram party arrived Louella busied herself with a plan of escape to see her lover. Indulged by Grace Poole, the large wooden chest in Louella's chambers contained an assortment of dresses and clothes, including a maid's uniform that Louella would sometimes wear to brush her jailor's hair and pretend to wait on her. This evening, determined and desperate to see John, Louella donned the gown, apron and cap pertinent to a junior ladies maid and as soon as Grace's snores indicated she was safe to slip away into the night she did just that hurrying through the corridors of the Hall, as if on some urgent ladies' business. As just another new face in a sea of new faces, she was thus able to move around the Hall unseen.

Adding opiate drops to Grace's evening gin allowed Louella to slip away just after nine. That night, in his cottage, John had a surprise for her. When she arrived he had removed her dress, leaving only her underclothes and her naked feet. Upstairs in his chamber, lit by candles and the moon streaming in through the window, John studied Louella's feet against the wooden floor. Adorned with gold rings, there was a neat beauty to their nakedness with her petite toes and slender ankles. As his master had kept her without shoes for ten years after burning her footwear on the pyre in the garden soon after her arrival, John half expected her feet to be dirty and coarse, but he knew, from the way she had run her feet and toes over his naked body, that they were as soft and sweet as the full lips she kissed him with.

John would not have kept his horses without shoes and nor would he see his lover left unshod. When last in town, John had arranged to order a pair of ladies hunting boots from the bootmaker there. As it was not unusual for the coachman to order such items for the ladies of the house via instructions from a ladies maid, his request was not considered remarkable and no comment was made. Besides, it was well known locally that there was talk afoot regarding the likelihood of Mr Rochester announcing his forthcoming engagement to Blanche Ingram, therefore everyone simply assumed that the boots were for one of the ladies in his party.

In front of the fire, by candlelight, in the snug of his cottage, John laid out brown paper, charcoal and twine. He gently lifted Louella's foot and guided it to the paper, stroking her slowly from her delicate ankle to her pretty toes with his fingers. The charcoal made an easy pattern, gliding smoothly over the paper as he carefully drew around each delicate foot. Then, using the twine, he measured the length of her legs and their width in three places, marking these carefully on the pattern and securing the twine with wax to the paper.

As Louella stood, watching John bending over her feet with such tenderness, she understood that he was giving her back what Mr Rochester had taken from her. More than just her shoes. Her freedom. Her husband had stolen not just her liberty, but her life as she had known it. And by stealing her liberty he had stolen her future. Looking at John now, Louella knew, with absolute certainty, by his act of love and compassion, that not only did she now have a future, but that this future could be real. She had stared at the walls of her prison on the third floor so often and for so long there had been times when her future seemed so dark and so bleak that when she looked into it she saw nothing. All that had changed. John's embrace had brought her back to life. In his arms she found that life had new meaning. His kisses had healed her past and become her future, every prospect of which now contained in its detail the man who knelt before her.

His work done, John carefully set aside his tools, and raising himself on his knees to half his height, pulled Louella towards him. Wrapping his arms around her waist he buried his head in the soft mound of her stomach and held her tightly for a few moments before slowly sliding his hands under her skirts and up to the smooth skin of her thighs. He felt her quiver, not just from his touch, but from the anticipation of the caresses that she knew would follow. John couldn't help but touch Louella. Every part of her fascinated him. Nothing was too intimate. The line of her leg, the curve of her calf, the arch of her back and the bend of her neck. All captivated him. He had never met a woman like her. Never met a woman who held his attention so completely, and with whom he could feel so much like a man. She made no demands upon him, nor did she judge him. In the night she would joyfully give herself to him, and in that gift of love he, too, would take her and make her his own, again and again until she had had the best of him and he had nothing left to give.

Still standing on the wooden floor with John kneeling at her feet, Louella bent forwards to caress his hair and kiss his head. She ran her fingers through his mane and, holding his face gently in her hands, bent his head upwards so she could look at him. His eyes were gentle with emotion. Raising himself to his full height, their positions reversed, Louella now looked up into John's eyes. As she pushed her body against his, he kissed her. Deeply. Forcefully. An act of possession that echoed his desire to be inside her. Sighing, she yielded to the mutuality of their mounting impatience, leaning into him and surrendering her body to his. They held on to the moment. More than just a lover's kiss. Two souls entwined. Two halves becoming one. Each completed by the other. Whole at last. With his memories of what was to come, of how she would look and how she would taste, John took Louella by the hand and gently led her up the stairs to bed.

• • • •

As Coachman, John was responsible for making small running repairs for the carriage harness, saddlery and leather bridle work of the horses. It was a skill his father had taught him, passed down from father to son through the generations of Estate workers that had served the Rochester family. Once a piece of harness leather has been cut and shaped, the edges are stained and then rubbed with beeswax to seal them. The stain is a brown vegetable dye mixed with pearl glue and water then heated over a fire to melt the glue and fix the colour. Even in the rain, the colour could not be rubbed off.

John had a ready supply of edge stain and pearl glue, prepared for any small repairs that might be needed. In the morning, at Louella's insistence, he gave her some of the liquid in a small brown pottery jar. She needed it she said, for her painting. Wrapping the jar in rags, she carried it carefully back up to the third floor. Sneaking herself back into her rooms she locked the door from the inside and hid the jar amongst the paints in the corner of the room that caught the afternoon sun, and where she knew that it would not be noticed. Grace Poole slept on. A heavy stupor that would gradually lift with snorts and grunts as the house also awoke and came back to life.

Slipping off her clothes, Louella crawled into bed. Tired but happy from her night with John, she welcomed the chance to rest her body and sleep. But sleep would not come. Thoughts and ideas swirled around in her head. Fragments of the future. Disconnected as yet with no storyline to link them together. The golden thread of time not yet woven around them. A plan half made. Half thought. As the sun finally lifted itself from the ground and began its lazy passage across the sky, Louella sighed and once more imagining John's loving embrace in that safe place where she held her memories of him, she closed her eyes and slept.

Chapter 17

Lisa's previous article on the different kinds of sex within relationships had been published by *Psychologies Magazine*. Caroline Harvey had sent an email to ask for another piece, this time on 'How to identify the perfect partner'. Being currently single and not in a relationship, the irony of the request was not lost on Lisa. Perhaps by writing the article she would be able to learn for herself what it was she really wanted in a man. She often found the process of writing therapeutic in the sense that it helped her to clarify her own thoughts, so, taking a notebook and pen from her desk, she closed down the computer and decided to go and sit in one of the secluded university college gardens. She would take some fruit and water, find herself a shaded spot under a tree where she could smell the fragrance of roses and imagine herself in the arms of her perfect man. By imagining herself in the future, with the vantage point of retrospect, perhaps she could look backwards over time and write about how she had arrived there. So with the late morning sun high in the sky and the grass underfoot already dry, with time to daydream, Lisa stepped out into the sunshine and into her future.

Settled under her favourite tree in the Scholars' Garden of Clare College, Lisa continued to think about relationships. More specifically, that key relationship with someone so special it's possible to settle down to create and share a life with them. What is so important about the dynamics between two people that makes them choose each other, she wondered? Assuming that it's possible to live a happy and fulfilled life with many people rather than waiting in hope for 'The One', how can we identify the perfect partner? Is it about looks, wondered Lisa? Although physical attraction is undoubtedly important within a relationship, she dismissed looks as the starting point as being far too shallow. Then she remembered something her mother had told her:

"Darling, you need to understand that men learn to love the woman they fancy, whereas women learn to fancy the man they love".

So perhaps looks and attraction are more important than she first thought, particularly for men. Or is it about being successful? Are we attracted to people who are successful, as being specially chosen by them somehow makes us become successful too? But what does success mean? Is someone successful if they are rich? Or are they successful if they love their life and are happy, regardless of how much money they have? People are complex and infinitely connected across all areas of their lives. Lisa considered that all of these things and more must in some way combine to create a whole package. So perhaps thinking about the whole package rather than 'just' the person would be a better place to start.

When you are identifying your 'perfect partner', what you are effectively doing is recreating your future. So before you start thinking about the 'right' person to share your life, perhaps it's a good idea to identify the kind of life that you want to lead. For example, do you want to live in the city, the suburbs or the countryside? Do you prefer the sophistication of the theatre and ballet or the simple pleasures of an evening meal and a quiet drink in your local pub? Do you want a life with children or without them? If you want children do they need to be your own or would you be prepared to be a step-parent?

How important is money to you? Do you want to live in luxury with no money worries or do you take a more pragmatic approach and feel that 'having enough' would make you happy? What kind of house would you like to live in? Brick, stone or wood? A detached new executive home, a Victorian pile or a cosy cottage that's two hundred years old? Do you want pets and animals? Chickens, a dog, a cat, a horse or would you prefer the tranquil calm of tropical fish? Or perhaps you would prefer a pristine home in various shades of cream with no animals in sight? Would you prefer modern minimalist or cosy clutter? Of course none of these questions or your answers to them will be set in stone and the type of environment you want to create for yourself in your ideal future is entirely up to you. You can dare to dream. By identifying your ideal lifestyle you will be able to notice what it is that you are prepared to compromise on, or even let go of should the right person come along.

When you understand the environment and lifestyle you want to create for yourself in your ideal world, you will be in a better position to find someone to share it with you. You might even find them along the way as you create your new lifestyle and your new life. So the question is, do you want that person to be just like you? Someone who wants the same things in life as you do, or someone who compliments you? They could be similar to you in some ways and different in others, or they might be completely different to you. Difference in a partner can be exciting; however, it can also lead to conflict, disagreement and misunderstandings. Therefore, you might decide, on balance, that you would prefer someone who is similar to you in that they share your beliefs and values.

The next thing you might want to think about, and this relates to the 'type' of person you would want your ideal partner to be, is which personality characteristics are important to you? There are more than a hundred personality traits which are probably best described as being our personal characteristics that we display more or less of such as kindness or shyness or our particular preference for risk-taking. These don't operate in isolation, but combine to create a unique personality profile that is 'us'. Of course we change over time, but unless we embark on a programme of active self-development, our personality characteristics tend to be fairly stable over time.

Lisa stopped writing. This was complicated. She needed to find a way of helping her readers to understand and explore personality traits more easily. Perhaps a list identifying the advantages and disadvantages of each trait would help. It would be a long list and not really suitable for inclusion in the article, but perhaps the magazine could include the list on their website and people could print off an ideal partner profile. That would show them more easily whether they want someone who is just like them or is different from them. It would encourage people to identify those particular personality characteristics that they value in a partner, and was something that a few of the more sophisticated internet dating sites were keen on such as match.com and eHarmony. She would ask Caroline what she thought of the idea.

But what about chemistry thought Lisa. It's all very well sharing beliefs and values, but that spark of sexual chemistry between two people has to be there. Without it there is no passion. Passion within an intimate relationship had to be there for her, although she recognised that not everyone is as interested in, or motivated by, passion. Without passion to leave you breathless, an intimate relationship lacks intimacy somehow. Lisa wasn't sure if this was the easiest part of the relationship jigsaw puzzle or the most difficult. How do you identify sexual chemistry or do you just notice when it isn't there? Is it the way someone looks to you or the way they look at you?   Is it how you feel when they touch you or the anticipation of their touch?   Is it to do with the smell and taste of someone or is it how they make you feel when you are together?   Is sexual chemistry something that can be learnt or taught?   Or rather, is it either just there or not there?

Lisa thought about a man she had once met and dated briefly called Chris.   A lovely guy.   Beautiful blue eyes, an easy smile, a great sense of humour, good with children and animals, kind, intelligent, generous, fun to be with and good looking.   Then when she kissed him for the first time ... there was nothing.   Just nothing. And it was the same for him.   When he had kissed her he had immediately known that she wasn't the woman for him.   Her physical and sexual response to him just didn't match his blueprint of the ideal woman.   But what had interested Lisa most wasn't the lack of sexual chemistry between them, it was that they had both known, instinctively and immediately, that the sexual chemistry was missing.   Rather than the sexual chemistry being mutually present, it had been mutually absent.   As a woman, and disappointing as the kiss had been, that mutual recognition had been fascinating.   As she hadn't seen Chris again after their first, and last, kiss, she hadn't been able to talk to him about it.   However, it had been an interesting experience and she would no doubt be a better psychologist and a more understanding woman because of it.

With her thoughts returning to the article, Lisa wondered what someone would do with a list of the personality characteristics of their ideal partner.   A flat list on a piece of paper was a long way from a person made of flesh and blood with their own desires and needs, and naturally their own idea of an ideal partner.   But is it really a good idea to have a 'shopping list' for an ideal partner? What happens if they ticked most of the boxes but not all of them?

To contemplate this thought for a while Lisa put her notes to one side, stood up to stretch, and spent ten minutes walking around the garden, smelling the fragrant scent of the roses and marvelling at the beauty of nature. Lisa often found that taking a walk helped her to think things through, and after taking a few sips of water from the bottle in her hand she settled down once again under the trees with her notepad to continue writing. A number of thoughts had occurred to her as she had been walking around. Firstly, a list is not definitive. It was a set of guidelines only; guidelines that could be reviewed and added to over time. And of course, certain things which seem important at a certain time in one's life might seem less important at a later date.

She also thought that some of the things on the list would be more important than others. So perhaps reviewing the list periodically and prioritising those things that are really important would be useful. For example, Lisa considered kindness and generosity as crucial characteristics in her ideal man, and anyone who was either selfish, arrogant, narcissistic, overly critical or derogatory about others would very soon be shown the door. Lisa thought a little more about those things that might be on her own list. It occurred to her that for some reason, and she wasn't quite sure why, it was important to her that any boyfriend enjoyed the work that he did and was good at it. It wouldn't matter to her whether he was an investment banker, a carpenter, an artist or a gardener. Nor would it matter how much he earned. What was important she decided, was that he woke every morning and looked forward to his day.

Surprised at how short her list was, she didn't really care what her ideal man looked like just so long as she fancied him. Nor would it matter whether he was American, European, African or

Inuit. Someone who looked like James Dean, Brad Pitt or Hugh Jackman would be nice, but passion could strike in the most unlikely of places she thought, smiling at the idea of finding an attractive and traditionally dressed Inuit walking through the streets of Cambridge.

Lisa thought that she certainly wanted someone who was good with children and animals. After all, she hoped to be able to enjoy both one day. Someone who was good with his hands would be nice. She enjoyed decorating and DIY and making things for her home, so a partner who could share that with her would make them more of a partnership. A team. As a post-grad student who wasn't a member of one of the many 'varsity sports clubs, she lived rather a solitary life. Expected to study, research and write alone, she would really like to feel part of a team. Reviewing her list for a final time, she noticed it was three thirty. Time for tea. She would end the article by suggesting that its readers have the courage to create their own ideal lives first and trust that once they had done so, the 'perfect' partner would appear and want to share it with them. Her own checklist would be a useful guide to help her recognise her own Mr Right, – just in case he didn't look like Brad Pitt!

Chapter 18

Louella loved the way that John looked at her. John's eyes didn't see a mad woman, a rejected wife, a lost sister or any of the other roles she had played in her life. When John looked at her he saw only the woman. A beautiful woman. His woman. A woman he had taken for his own pleasure and made his own. When John looked upon Louella's dusky countenance, he felt more like a man, and she in turn, felt more like a woman. In his company and under his gaze she felt satisfied, happy, relaxed, safe and confident with a deep sense of contentment as if she had finally found her place in the world. Everything she had ever wanted she had found in his arms. Finally, she had found her place and her peace.

Although he didn't say it often, Louella knew that she was loved by John. As a man of few words, his tender touch and passionate kisses when he held her in his arms spoke more to Louella than volumes of poetry and pretty verse. From the first moments of meeting their courtship had been physically charged; initially a meeting of bodies rather than minds, they were also matched in intellect and both felt easy and secure in the company of the other.

In equal measure John felt loved by Louella and delighted in her company. Her sighs in his arms, the light touch of her fingertips up and down his spine, her willing embrace and the way she held onto him tightly while she slept told him all he needed to know about their union. In the times they spent together there was never a void between them. When they walked in the gardens of Thornfield Hall or the fields of the Estate, their touches were tender and playful; an outward sign of the emotional and sexual bond between them. But Louella knew her time with John was a stolen season, knew also that Mr Rochester would never willingly let her go. Accordingly, she, too, began to plan their escape.

Whilst the Ingram party was present in the house and her husband distracted by Blanche Ingram's obvious charms, Louella was free to see John often, which naturally was every night she could slip away and escape from her prison. As she spent most of the night making love with John, consequently, she slept for most of the day. This pleased Grace Poole, but meant that early one evening through her windows she missed a very important visitor; a visitor who could change the course of her future completely. A man who, upon the first sight of him, made even Mr Rochester turn pale as he strode unexpectedly and uninvited into the privacy of the Master's library.

"Mason, my God man! What do you want with me? Haven't I done enough for you and your God-damned family already?"

"I have come to see her and take her home, Rochester. It's been ten years. You cannot incarcerate her forever."

"I can do as I please. I am Master here, Mason; do not tell me what I may or may not do with my own wife. She is my property and my responsibility damn her."

"Nevertheless, Rochester, I want to see her. I have come a long way, I will not be denied now. Give her to me; I will see you do right by her or be damned in Hell."

"I'm already in a living Hell. Very well, Mason, you may see her. Wait here, I will instruct Mrs Fairfax to find you a room. Join us for dinner, we will see her in the morning. We'll not disturb her tonight, you know how she can be."

With that the mysterious stranger joined the house party, much to the delight and excitement of the ladies who found his dark good looks and unusual accent a new and welcome distraction. He was subdued however, mostly lost in his own thoughts and largely ignored the flirtatious remarks of the young ladies who were always eager and on the lookout for compliments. All of the young ladies bar one, of course. The governess to Mr Rochester's ward was singular in her seriousness and would rarely be drawn into conversation, let alone seek or expect any kind of compliment.

Upstairs on the third floor and unaware of her visitor's arrival, Louella prepared herself for another night with her lover. Unlocking the door and about to step out into the corridor, she heard a man's footfall and quickly ran back into her chambers. She did not want her husband to catch her about to slip out. Waiting silently in her room, listening for the footsteps to recede along the corridor, she was immediately on her guard when instead they stopped outside and entered. Knowing that it would not be John and fearing her husband, Louella ran to her bed and sat on it, looking wildly at the door. But the man who entered her bedroom was neither John nor her husband; the man who met her eyes was her brother. Richard Mason stood before her, the legitimate white offspring of the union between old Mr Mason and his first wife.

In that moment Louella reflected on the life of her half-brother. Over-mastered by their father to the same extent that she and her sisters had been over-indulged by him, he had grown into a weak-willed man who lacked backbone and resilience. After their father died, he had quickly ruined the Jamaican Estate with a series of bad investments and subsequently followed her new husband around like a soul lost. The last ten years had been good to him, however; he had recovered some of the family's fortune, discovered a new confidence and appeared in Louella's chambers the image of his father as a young and vibrant man.

"Why 'ave you cum 'eer? Wot do you want wiv me?"

"Hello, Antoinetta, how are you? You look well. Regretfully, ... I need to inform you that your mother is gravely ill and has been asking for you. She is not long for this world."

"But why 'ave you cum 'eer? Wot do you want wiv me?"

"I have come to take you home."

"But thees is my 'ome. I 'av been 'eer ten years. 'Eee will neever let me go."

"I will speak with him. This is your chance to leave here, Antoinetta."

With these words Richard Mason crossed the floor of Louella's chamber and approached his half-sister as she sat on her bed. He held his arms open to embrace her, but she shrank from his advancing touch. Ignoring her obvious reticence, he embraced her regardless and held her to him tightly. Louella felt an overwhelming anger. How dare he come here now? Why now after leaving her to rot in England for ten years? How dare he come here and try to take her away from the one person who made her life bearable; the one person who made her life worth living. Oh how she hated him! Louella's anger boiled over. Volcanic in its heat she erupted finding a strength that took her brother completely by surprise.

"You peeg, I weel keel you. I 'ate you."

"Antoinetta, calm down."

"That ees not my name! Nor ees it Bertha wot ee calls me. My name ees Louella."

"Antoinetta, my sister, calm down, I have come to take you home."

"Nooooo. Geet off me. Leev me alone. My 'ome ees eer, I want to stay. I weel neever go wiv you."

These last words were screeched into the night air. Finding a fury within her hereto buried, Louella launched herself at her brother, biting and scratching at his face, body and clothes. Were she to have possessed a knife she would have run his heart through with it. As she did not own such an implement, she clawed at his skin in an apparent effort to reach his heart with her bare hands and tear it from his chest. Reaching across to the small table beside her bed and snatching the small pair of sharp nail scissors she found there,

Louella lashed out at her half-brother and stabbed him in the shoulder. Three inches lower, and she would indeed have stopped his heart.

"You witch, get off of me. You have killed me."

With rivulets of scarlet running down his face and his shirt rapidly becoming sticky with his own lifeblood, Richard threw off his half-sister and staggered towards the door. Picking herself up from the floor, Louella went to follow him and attack him again but was prevented from doing so by Grace Poole. Aroused by Louella's screams at her brother, Mrs Poole used her body weight to restrain Louella as one would an unruly child, wrapping her arms around Louella's chest and pinning her arms to her sides. Grace Poole need not have worried however, her anger spent, Louella had slid once again onto the wooden floor and now sobbed uncontrollably. She was a sorry sight to behold, with her dress spattered in blood and her brother's flesh hanging from beneath her fingernails.

Knowing better than to leave her charge alone after such an eventful evening, Grace Poole stayed awake with her late into the night, protecting her against her husband's inevitable visit and assuring him that Richard Mason had been the protagonist having entered the rooms of his own accord, unbidden and uninvited. How else had he been near enough to his sister for her to attack him in such a way? Especially, she assured him, as his loyal and faithful servant she was with her charge night and day. Caring little for her assurances, the Master of Thornfield Hall quickly strode away. Having sent a servant for the doctor, he had left his brother-in-law to the careful ministrations of the meek and mild governess whom he had sworn to secrecy about the incident. More than anyone else of his acquaintance, Edward Fairfax Rochester knew in the core of his soul that was his very essence, that he could rely on Jane Eyre.

Shortly afterwards, and predictably without his sister, Richard Mason left Thornfield Hall in the company of the doctor who would care for him until he was fully recovered. He did not plan to return to the Estate in his sister's lifetime.

After Richard's visit and Louella's subsequent attack upon her brother, Mr Rochester's mood changed and shortly afterwards the Ingram party were sent on their way. Blanche's mother, having hoped for an announcement of impending nuptials, was disappointed, but consoled herself with the thought that the distance between their two houses was of little consequence to an ardent suitor. Mr Rochester visited neither his wife nor Blanche Ingram, however, preferring to stay at Thornfield in the quiet and gentle company of Adèle's Mademoiselle Eyre.

It was not long before the long-awaited announcement of a wedding surprised even the usually unflappable housekeeper, Mrs Fairfax. The Master was to take a wife: a slip of a girl almost half his age. Both deliriously happy in the other's company, they spent every waking minute together. Mrs Fairfax could understand entirely why the Master would choose such an amenable bride, but was at a loss to understand why Jane Eyre, a young woman with no regard for fortune, would want to marry a man twice her age with a reputation for women and a violent temper. She loyally kept her thoughts to herself however, and genuinely wished them every happiness.

Determined to have his own way and take Jane as his wife regardless of the consequences, so as not to break the magical spell he found himself under, Edward Fairfax Rochester avoided the third floor and thus all reminders of his wife and his previous life with her. For those of you who know the story of *Jane Eyre*, the following tale will come as no surprise.

On the eve of the wedding, with her costume for the morrow already laid out in her room ready for its wearer, Jane ate a few bites of an early supper and waited for the return of her husband-to-be, called away on business the night before. It was gone nine and he would not return until eleven o'clock had passed. Upon her Master's return and after a second supper, at which Jane could not eat even one mouthful, they talked by candlelight in the warmth of the fire, neither wishing to be parted from the other. After the clock struck midnight, and at Mr Rochester's insistence, Jane recounted the events of the previous night, telling him a story that sent the sharp sword of terror through her fiancé's heart, making him insist that for the remainder of the night his beloved slept with Adèle in the nursery.

The previous night Jane had been woken by the prospect and countenance of a woman she described as, *"the Vampyre"*. A woman with long dark hair and swollen and grotesque features who had tried Jane's wedding veil on in front of the mirror before renting it in two and trampling it on the floor. A savage and ghastly woman, barefoot and dressed in a long white nightgown. A woman Jane had never seen before. A woman Jane insisted was not Grace Poole despite Mr Rochester's insistence of the fact. Of course, dear reader, we know very well that the woman in white was not Grace Poole. The ghostly apparition Jane Eyre met for the first time that night was the woman we know as Louella.

But why? Why had Louella gone to Jane's room and torn asunder the very representation of marriage? What thoughts had driven her to the second floor? With her husband evidently away, why had she spent time stalking her rival rather than in her lover's arms? She had not hurt Jane in any way, despite holding a candle to her face and examining the terrified governess who had fainted through fear. A petrified Jane had seen a grotesque spectre, not the gentle woman of John's experience.

Naturally, Louella's perspective was very different. Having heard of the impending nuptials she was delighted to think that she would finally be free of the tyranny of marriage to Edward Fairfax Rochester. Divorce was unusual, but not unheard of. No-one had spoken to her of it, however, and she worried, not unreasonably given the circumstances, that her husband would poison her and do her in before his marriage to the young, naïve and entirely innocent governess. Consequently, not trusting Grace Poole, Louella had eaten and drunk very little for the previous few weeks, relying only on John's larder for sustenance. She had gone to Jane's room on a whim, determined to see for herself in close-up, the blameless virgin who was to replace her.

After sending Jane to the relative safety of the nursery in the company of his ward Adèle, Mr Rochester fled to the third floor. He wanted to be certain of the whereabouts of the detested millstone round his neck that weighed so heavily and threatened to choke the very breath of life from him. Finding two sleeping people as expected in the chambers he retreated downstairs locking the door securely behind him, but not before leaving Grace Poole a note with some little instruction regarding the following day. He could not, indeed would not sleep, and spent the remainder of the night pacing the corridors of the house, on guard against the demons and monsters of his mind. In a few more hours he would be married to Jane. Bigamously, it was true, but married nevertheless. Married and out of the country by nightfall!

As early as was decent, Edward Rochester ordered Mrs Fairfax to wake Jane and requested that Sophie, the French maid who normally cared for Adèle, should dress her. There was to be no wedding breakfast, no celebration, not in this house. As soon as they were married, he would secrete his bride in the coach and John would take them across country to the nearest port. From there, they would travel on to Europe and the safety of those countries where no-one cared who they were or from whence they came.

In a hurry to reach the church that stood, silently awaiting their patronage, just beyond the gates of Thornfield Hall, Mr Rochester almost ran there towing Jane in his wake, her tiny hand in his. Thinking he was safe in the church, he began to relax. But his relief was both presumptuous and premature. The wicked deed was not yet done; his plan not yet concluded. On the instruction and in the company of Richard Mason, a certain Mr Briggs, a London lawyer, had been dispatched to the church to stop the ceremony.

"Mr Rochester has a wife now living".

Thwarted in the last minutes of the service in his attempt to ruin Jane's reputation under the guise of his own happiness, Edward Fairfax Rochester took the assembly back to the Hall and up to the third floor. In accordance with the instruction her Master had left earlier that morning, Grace Poole had doubled the dose of the opiate drugs she had previously used so often to subdue Louella. As a consequence, her charge now paced the corner of the room, snarling and whining, talking to herself and crying out at the hallucinations that so tormented her. An unwilling actress on a stage of her husband's making; her audience the gathered congregation.

Chapter 19

It's all very well meeting a great guy who ticks all of your boxes, but then what? How do you know whether your new and exciting relationship is going to work out? Psychologists have been studying relationships for some time and their research has identified certain markers within a couple's communication style that can predict the success, or otherwise, of their relationship in the long term. So what are these markers? What are the things that indicate whether a relationship is going to work, and, as importantly, what are the early clues that it is not going to work?

According to John Gottman of the Relationship Research Institute in Seattle, successful couples say yes to each other much more than they say no. They use what's called positive language patterns; looking for agreement and for ways to accentuate the good things about each other and their relationship. They say things like *"Yes, that's a good idea ... Yes, I agree, let's do that ... What do you think? ...* (and) *That would be nice, thank you"*.

Interestingly, as a quality, kindness tops men's lists as well as women's in terms of the personality characteristic that they most want in a partner. Apart from being nice to each other, couples whose relationship is most likely to survive life's natural ups and downs are supportive of each other in public as well as in private. They don't tend to make a decision without talking it through with their partner first and they also share lots of small moments of intimacy and togetherness that reinforce the connection between them and set them apart from other people, thereby emphasising their 'coupleness'. Observers can see very clearly from the looks and close moments they share, that these two people are 'a unit'.

Gottman and his colleagues also found that a couple's disagreement strategy could provide a critical indicator of the likelihood that a relationship would either be successful or would end. After more than thirty-five years of studying relationships, so powerful is their research, they now claim that just by observing a couple in a room for fifteen minutes, they can predict, with a very high degree of accuracy, whether the couple will still be together in five years time.

Within one of the research experiments, they give each couple a simple task to do, such as taking an assortment of materials like paper, tape, string and scissors and being asked to build a tower that is freestanding, strong and beautiful, within thirty minutes. Researchers observe how the couple communicate and how they disagree. It turns out that a couple's disagreement strategy is just as important as their agreement strategy.

Everyone is different in terms of the amount of disagreement they feel comfortable with. Some people seem naturally better able to cope with more conflict than others. However, even couples with a high level of conflict can be successful in their relationship, provided that they have the right supportive strategies in place to balance their high conflict style. Couples who avoid conflict can also be successful. The problems occur when there's a mismatch in the levels of conflict that each person prefers and they then have different, or poor, strategies for resolving that conflict. Film and television writers are particularly aware of the process of disagreement and are very good at writing realistic conflict scenes. It provides much of the content for romantic comedies, dramas and soap operas.

So what is an effective and helpful disagreement strategy? Is there such a thing? It turns out that there is. Firstly, it's useful to recognise that disagreeing with someone is a process; it has a beginning, a middle and an end. The beginning of a disagreement is obviously how a conflict starts; its trigger point. Conflict rarely starts by accident. Some people seem to pick fights or create them for some reason. Sometimes it's by saying no, or the tone of voice or even a look that is responded to negatively. Sometimes it's an imagined slight or a difference of opinion, and sometimes it's someone lashing out because something or someone else has upset them and the disagreement has nothing whatsoever to do with their partner. People can really be quite creative when it comes to initiating argument!

Secondly, how someone quarrels is as important as what they are disagreeing about. This ongoing confrontation, the to and fro table tennis of conflict is what gives an argument its energy and keeps it going, like all rallies, sometimes for quite a while. If you have been through the experience of a divorce, you will be very aware of this stage. Many couples, due to issues such as power, control, lashing out after a perceived hurt or trying to protect their own sense of self, find themselves stuck in the rally stage of conflict where all efforts at reconciliation are rejected and batted straight back with each player keeping a score of the points that they've won and lost.

The third and final stage of a conflict is its resolution. This includes not just how the disagreement is brought to a close, but also those steps that are taken to repair any damage that may have been done to the relationship by the conflict itself. Gottman paid particular attention to stage three in his research. He was interested in which one of the couple would be the first to offer an olive branch in an attempt to end the disagreement and repair the relationship. In successful and happy couples there was no pattern, with each person being willing to apologise. The repair attempt was always accepted and humour often played a part. In unsuccessful couples, that is, in couples who ultimately parted, there was a pattern of one person usually being the first to offer up the olive branch which was often rejected by their partner, at least initially. Lashing out, sulking, refusing to communicate and not apologising were all yet more examples of a poor disagreement style and ultimately predictors of a relationship that was highly unlikely to succeed in the long term.

In essence, the indicators of a healthy and happy relationship are kindness, humour, respect and admiration, with respect and admiration on both sides being critical. The indicators of an unhealthy relationship are a lack of respect, criticism or worse, contempt. Contempt and criticism are highly destructive as they communicate disgust. Contempt and criticism destroy relationships, but before they do, they make the people within that relationship profoundly unhappy. Unhappiness causes changes in someone's immune system, and it is this dis-ease that can so often lead to illness of some kind or another. Of course this is only one part of the jigsaw puzzle of our health; nutrition, exercise and even our genetic inheritance are also critically important.

In healthy relationships, be they friendships, professional working relationships among colleagues, relationships with family members or within a romantic couple, there is a 'generosity of spirit' in the relationship that influences all of the interactions between them. There is an acknowledgement, although this is often unconsciously recognised rather than deliberately said, that the emotional and physical wellbeing of someone else is important to you. In close relationships, there may be times when the emotional and physical wellbeing of another person is even more important to you than your own.

When you put someone else's wants or needs above your own, you make what the glorious Italians call "*I sacrifice*", or sacrifices for them. That may be a mother feeding her family before herself and going hungry, or a family giving up a new car or a family holiday to send a child to university or help out another family member. Some of these sacrifices may be quite small and others considerably bigger. What unites them all, however, is that they are freely given, and moreover, given with love and compassion.

Just as there are many different kinds of relationships, there are also many different kinds of love. The universal translation of *"Your physical and emotional wellbeing is important to me"* is, *"I love you"*. Simple in its message, yet complicated in its meaning, and much misunderstood, particularly if people make the mistake of thinking that all love is romantic love which it clearly is not.

So how can we surround ourselves with loving friendships and relationships that energise and nourish us rather than diminish or hurt us? Firstly, and most importantly, we need to examine the relationship that we have with ourselves. We cannot truly love others if we don't also love ourselves. To love others and not ourselves is to have an unhealthy relationship which, whether we recognise it or not, is actually toxic and, will, like chemical waste in the soil, seep into the water table of our own wellbeing.

Often of course, it is easier to focus on someone else rather than focusing on ourselves, particularly if we don't actually like ourselves very much. But if we really loved someone, would we say the things to them that we say to ourselves in the privacy of our own heads? Would we set such high standards for them or punish them for not being the superwoman or superman the media seems to suggest that we should be? No, we wouldn't. We would be kind to them. We would be quick and generous in our praise and we would be equally quick to support and forgive them, just as we would be to a child. That's what's meant by, 'feeding your inner child'. It's not narcissistic, it's nourishing and giving generously to the most important relationship that we will ever have; the relationship that we have with ourselves.

As for 'toxic' relationships, these are any relationships that don't nourish and support us to be our best selves. They are easily recognised simply because they make us feel badly about ourselves and our lives in some way rather than making us feel better. If you find yourself in a toxic relationship or you recognise that some of your friendships are toxic, you need to find the courage either to transform those relationships if you can or, if you can't, to end them. If the relationship is important enough to you, you may be able to transform it by being honest, by being compassionate and by being a role model for a successful disagreement strategy. If the other person is unwilling to learn or simply doesn't want to change and have a healthy relationship with you, you may need to let them go and limit your contact with them. They may regret the ending of your relationship and try to reignite the flames of friendship, but if you do not want to do that, they will soon move on and spend time with other people who match their, unhealthy, emotional needs better than you do.

Transforming unhealthy relationships takes emotional courage, compassion, patience, the generosity of spirit to forgive, and the ability to be assertive, which is to recognise that your needs are as important as someone else's. Not more important and not less important, but equally as important, especially where kindness and respect are concerned. Within a couple, only once you have a healthy relationship can you go on to create a 'sacred space'; that special bond that is the Holy Grail of all romantic relationships.

Chapter 20

Mr Rochester could not sleep that night. Pacing his room for hours he had twice visited the third floor to remonstrate with his wife, comparing her to the young woman he had so very nearly made his own earlier in the day. How he wished that Bertha Mason were dead. How he wished that he had never set eyes on her, that she had never been born, that she had died like her own bastard offspring. He loathed the sight of her. How he wished that he was free to follow his wants and desires. All he wanted, all he desired, all he held dear in the world, was contained in the small and frail package that was Jane Eyre. His Jane. For she was his, every fibre in his being told him so. She had given herself up to him with her words and in her manner in ways equal to any physical union. A union that should have been his, this very night, and was now denied to him.

How he compared the two women. A juxtaposition of plainness and beauty, except that Jane Eyre had become beautiful in his eyes and his wife hideous. Oh, he could have gazed on Jane's countenance for a lifetime and never found it wanting in any element of loveliness. Jane's frailty in his arms only served to make him love her more. How she had struggled against him in the orchard a month before. How she had cried in his strong embrace, her passions let free at last, escaping into the night air as her tears slipped down her cheeks unchecked. How much he had loved her in that moment. He had vowed to protect her from the world, locking her in his arms and keeping her safe from any who would harm her.

A juxtaposition of intellect. He had found in Jane a willing and eager student, a powerful intelligence which would not be bowed by any argument from him. She did not flinch from his contentions, instead she welcomed and embraced them and joyfully laughed as she tested his mental powers. He had fallen madly and passionately in love with Jane's mind and also with her manners. From the first time he had met her in the lane when he had fallen from Mesrour and she had refused to leave his side until she had been of some service to him, he had known that she would do him good. He had found in Jane Eyre's tiny frame a brave and courageous spirit. An equal. An intellectual equal too and he took giddy pleasure in her mind, just as he had taken such pleasure in his wife's body ten years before.

Physically and mentally, the woman he would have made his second wife could not have been more different from the first. Emotionally, both were passionate creatures, but Jane repressed her passions and struggled against them with her will and strength of character as much as Bertha Mason embraced and embodied hers. A cultivated and genteel English garden rose, sweet smelling and delicate, compared to the untamed briars of the dog rose that grew wild and unchecked in the hedgerows. He would have her. He would have his Jane and be damned.

Leaving his room just as the dawn approached it shyly through the windows, Edward Fairfax Rochester made his way to his lover's room. Expecting to find it locked as he had instructed, he was concerned to see it ajar and strode in, half afraid of finding a mad woman within. Nothing. A lifeless space. A cold and empty chamber despite the embers of a fire glowing in the hearth. His Jane was gone. No trace of his little bird. No clue as to where she had flown. The pearls he had given her for their nuptials lay abandoned on the small dressing table, as he himself had now been abandoned by her. In one breath he ran down the sweeping stairs to the front door and out onto the drive. Nothing. The dawn was still. No sign of her. He ran on. Down the gravel drive to the ornate iron gates that divided the Estate from the road. An empty landscape. Crying out her name, he sank to his knees as the birds sang their chorus of joy for the new day. He would have shot every last damn one of them to get his Jane back. But by her own hand she was gone.

• • • •

Almost as if he felt he were being punished for his bigamous intentions and that he deserved no such judgement, he bore his loss violently and without remorse. He would have taken a naïve and innocent virgin, the one thing he loved most in the world and, through his own selfish desires, have ruined it forever. By running away from him and all that he represented, Jane had saved herself, although that thought gave her no satisfaction. She was more moral than her master. A better woman than he was a man. She had escaped him and he deserved to be punished. The thought of her with another man drove him wild with jealousy. He would rather she was dead on the moors than in the arms of another. If he had been more than half a man, he would have found them and killed them both. His moods swung from violent and passionate rages to withdrawn melancholy. Then, only in the thought of finding his Jane again could he find the strength to rise from his bed and dress each day. The Estate continued around him. Winter turned to spring. He could see the bursting of new life and smell it in the air. Only these gave him hope that with the dawning of a new season he might see his Jane again.

Mr Rochester was a broken man. Utterly desolate. Inconsolable. Mad with the grief of lost hopes and dreams. His equal, Jane, had thwarted him. A better strategist than he, (for his strategy to make her his wife had failed in its employ), he was shattered. A fragmented and splintered mirror, which, even when repaired, would never be the same.

For months he stalked the corridors of Thornfield Hall revisiting every seat and every corner where they had spent time together. He relived his conversations with her again and again in his mind, talking to her memory and demanding that it submit to his will and return Jane to him. He was savage in his grief, his usual short temper replaced by such a morose fury that even the servants avoided him, and he spent his time alone with only Pilot for company.

His every waking moment and all of his dreams were filled with thoughts of Jane. He pounded the gardens in a desperate attempt to feel closer to her. Her presence had calmed him, without her he was violent. Dangerous. Brutal. An animal pacing the bars of its cage. Wild and unpredictable. In the garden, the burnt stump of the lightening tree became his refuge, linked with Jane by the memory of their first kiss and his teasing proposal to her. Oh happy moment, when she had finally agreed to become his. But how he remembered his prophetic words, how he wished he had never given them life.

"You complete me, little bird. How easily I could crush you, yet how bravely you stand your ground. But take care, Jane. I am the wolf to your Red Riding Hood".

She had bravely replied that she was not afraid and that the wolf was savage only because it hungered. She would feed it, she said, from her own fair hand, just as they had shared the picnic by the river that very day. By her hand her wolf would never feel hunger again.

But this wolf hardly ate. Hardly slept. Her memory haunted him and he would not be free of it. He was a man starving. Jane was a meal he could never eat, a thirst he could never quench. Physically, his body ached for her with a passion that was all consuming. Mentally, he heard her voice in his head, relived previous conversations with her and imagined new ones. Emotionally, he felt as if he would never be whole again. His only brief respite came with the drugs he took from his first wife's chambers. Better at least to lose himself in his memories of Jane than to live with the emptiness of a life without her, raw and cold.

In his study, he wrote endless letters instructing solicitors to search for her in every school and every private house in the country, but none had heard of Jane Eyre. He followed every whisper of a lead, but each led nowhere. He roamed the country on horseback willing her to appear from the hedgerow and startle his horse once again, so she could put her arm around him and rescue him from himself. But it was not to be. He found no trace of her. Nothing to bring him comfort. Nothing to give him hope.

The Master of Thornfield Hall rarely left his domain. A life spent in waiting. Waiting for Jane to return to him or a courier to bring some word of her. The house became his prison and he its jailor. A prison of his own making. He could not bear the sight of his ward, Adèle. The daughter of his French mistress, abandoned by her fickle mother, her need for a Governess had brought Jane to him. But now her endless tears for Madame left him unmoved. She was quickly dispatched to school. He knew not where and cared less. Without Jane, life had lost its meaning. There was no pleasure in the world, only pain. No joy, only grief. No solace could be his. Only the passionate and desperate hope of seeing her once again drove him to continue living each day. His body ached for her like a mother's body aches for its child. Totally. Completely. Utterly. A missing appendage without which he could not be complete. He lived one second at a time, one breath at a time. Every minute an eternity without her. He lived a half life. No solace could be his. Like the burnt and ravaged stump in the orchard, he was a remnant of the proud and vital man he had once been.

Chapter 21

The psychologist, Harold Rausch, who studied relationships at the University of Massachusetts, identified that couples differ in the amount of 'emotional distance' they prefer within their relationship. Just as we differ in the amount of conflict we feel comfortable with, it seems that we differ, too, in how emotionally close we want to feel to our partners.

Rausch saw emotionally distant couples as not being particularly interested in developing insights or a deep understanding of their relationship and of each other.   He described these couples, as a result of the distance between them, as being, 'emotionally brittle'; they only have an emotionally superficial, surface relationship.   In essence, they don't really talk, certainly not about anything fundamentally meaningful to them.   Their fragile and brittle emotional connection means that when problems and difficulties occur within the relationship, as they always will in our modern world, beset as it is by pressures and stresses, the couple will lack both the communication skills and the desire to resolve their problems.   Under pressure, their relationship will fracture and shatter like glass.

In terms of creating a deep and meaningful bond, a space where it's safe to be yourself, with all your hopes, dreams, weaknesses and foibles shared with another person, an emotionally distant relationship is problematic.   Perhaps it is fear that prevents us from becoming emotionally intimate.   Not everyone is brave enough to truly share themselves with someone else.   They feel emotionally exposed and vulnerable.   They are quite right, of course, being emotionally open and sharing ourselves intimately with someone else makes us vulnerable.   Loving someone gives them the power to hurt us. It's only by recognising that fact, trusting that they won't hurt us deliberately, whilst accepting that they might, and then forgiving them with love and compassion if they do, that enables us to have a truly intimate emotional relationship with both ourselves and our partner.

It's only once we are in a place of shared intimacy, vulnerability and trust, that we can create that special, 'sacred space' within our relationships. Making love within a sacred space is the Holy Grail of romantic relationships; it's a space where time and the rest of the world have no meaning. Time stands still, and yet there is all the time in the world. Being in a sacred space is about slowing down, about being completely present with ourselves and the person who is with us. Being in a sacred space is as much about the emotional connection between two people as it is about the sexual connection they share. In a sacred space, two people exist as individuals in the real and rational world, and yet they also exist to each other in the intimate, shared and private space that they have created between them.

Feeling safe in the space between you, so you can give all you have to offer, accept and receive all that the other person has to offer you, and be able to achieve your full potential as a person, both within your relationship, and also outside it, creates emotional and therefore chemical changes within you. Oxytocin is sometimes called the 'cuddle hormone'; it's what we create within our own bodies when we stroke and caress each other. It makes us more emotionally willing to trust others and also makes us feel closer to them. It's the reason why touch is so powerful.

Although you might think that the sacred space is only a place that lovers can share, nothing could be further from the truth.

Because it's about emotional intimacy, the sacred space between you can also be simply sitting together and reading the papers on a Sunday morning, easy in each other's company. Or it could be a shared lunch between two people who are genuinely good friends and who really like, love and respect each other in a reciprocal 'generosity of spirit' that is so very special. The Holy Grail of friendships is also this shared, sacred space. Between you, you have, together, created a place where you can truly 'be' yourselves, and it's this ultimate goal of authenticity that drives and motivates us all to become not only our true selves, but also to become our very best selves.

Chapter 22

By now an addict herself, their roles reversed, Grace Poole eagerly drank her evening gin and water then spoke for a while about her plans for a house in Plymouth. Louella encouraged her to talk, and refilled her glass twice more as the evening wore on. It was a night like any other; unremarkable, or so it seemed. By about ten o' clock 'Mrs' Poole was slumped, incoherent but still conscious, in the big chair. Encouraged by Louella to take one more drink, she slipped into silent oblivion. Louella looked at the prison warder who had now become her prisoner and untied the bunch of keys that hung around the sleeping woman's waist. Fetching from its hiding place amongst her paints, the small jar of dark brown liquid that John had so generously given her, Louella laid her captor down onto the rug on the wooden floor and deftly stripped her bare. Working quickly, Louella painted the comatose woman using the brown harness dye John had made up for her. Half an hour later the room contained not one, but two coffee-coloured creatures. Covering the intoxicated woman with a blanket to keep her warm and prolong her stupor Louella untied the tight bun on top of Grace's head and let her long hair flow loosely on the floor. This too was stained, covering all traces of grey, until, from a distance at least, you could almost think that the two women were sisters.

Dressing the unconscious form in a voluminous white nightgown, the kind she herself slept in, Louella stood up and reflected on her handiwork. She had planned this night for so long. She quickly dressed herself in her riding habit leaving her feet bare against the floor, her boots waiting for her with her lover in his cottage down the lane. Taking one of the candles, she slipped out of the room and along the unlit corridor. On her night time forays into the other world that had become her nocturnal reality, Louella had studied the layout of the house and considered most carefully what to do next. She knew exactly where to light the touch paper for maximum effect whilst still leaving herself a clear escape route via the servants' passageways that dissected the house.

Leaving flames licking at the curtains on the first and second floors Louella returned to her comatose jailor, still prostrate on the rug. Filling her pockets with what was left of her jewellery Louella made her final preparations. In the small next door chamber she found Grace Poole's savings, swollen by the sale of her own trinkets, secreted under her jailor's grubby mattress. She took them, folding the notes neatly and tucking them into her corset. Ready. Just one last thing.

Grace Poole awoke at some time past midnight, still delirious from the cocktail of drink and drugs and keen to find her bed. As Louella often wore clothes from her previous life, the fact that she was dressed at night in clothes made for travel went unnoticed. Louella led Grace up the stairs to the roof and guided her to the parapets at the front of the house where she let go of her jailor's hand for the last time. And as the homing pigeon is thrown into the air, Grace Poole was freed to her fate.

Drowning in the billowing and acrid smoke that filled the air, flames already engulfed the second floor and itched at the third. Frightened and confused, Grace Poole became hysterical and began screaming obscenities, running around the roof vainly searching for an escape route, but unable to find the door that would take her back to her room. The first Mrs Rochester slipped back to the hatch, hiding herself behind it when she heard her husband's imminent approach. Shouting and swearing at his wife and threatening to kill her himself because of the trouble she had caused, Mr Rochester stormed up onto the roof in the vilest of tempers. In a furious rage at the burning of his house and his home, of all that reminded him of Jane, Edward Fairfax Rochester strode about the parapets searching for his wife and calling her names.

Hiding in the smoke behind the egress, Louella escaped his tyranny and his temper for the last time, slipping unseen through the exit behind him and back into the corridor to safety. With one last look at the scene of destruction she had left behind her, Louella retraced her steps back to the first floor and fled the house.

Reader, you know the rest. Or at least, you think you do.

John was occupied in the stables. Knowing of Louella's plan and the timing of it, he had saved the horses although some of the carriages were not so fortunate. The house aflame, a raging orange inferno against the night sky, there was little anyone could do but stand and watch. There was shocked disbelief when an unknown figure in a billowing white night gown had leapt from the parapets, smashing itself almost beyond recognition on the ground below.

Injured in the fire and now unable to see, from the description of the coffee-coloured skin and the unkempt wild

129

dark hair, Mr Rochester had readily identified the broken body as that of his first wife, Antoinetta Bertha Mason, the real Mrs Rochester.

Louella waited for her lover at his cottage, naked in the marriage bed. Free at last, they held on to each other for strength as both shook at the enormity of what Louella had done. But what choice did she have? She had known, from the first tenderness of her breasts and the rising of nausea within her that, for the sake of her unborn child, she must somehow escape the tyranny of an estranged husband and her life as it had been. To give her child a future she knew that she must recreate her own. A mother's love. The ferocity of a protection more powerful than any lion's for its cubs. An honest love. And yet, a love so violent and powerful, it had led a gentle woman to murder in its name.

Louella lived with John as his wife for some time. Finally free and no longer a prisoner, to avoid questions from other Estate workers she remained hidden by day, willingly sitting in the cottage making those tiny clothes which she knew would serve her well in the months to come. Her belly and her breasts swelled. She had never been so happy. Never felt so whole or so complete. Days slipped into nights. Nights where she found her lover fuelled by the infatuation of impending fatherhood. Gentle. Tender. Passionate.

Louella and John lived a life of light and of laughter. Had they but known it, they felt alive equal in measure to the degree that Mr Rochester's life had been dulled. He lived in a world of darkness. Deadened by the pain of losing Jane, he hardly noticed the loss of his house or his hand. He was glad that she had left him, that she had escaped this fate. A blind cripple, he convinced himself that Jane would not want him now. And even if she lived, he would never again gaze on her lovely countenance, so what good were his eyes? He did not mourn their loss.

With the Hall a charred ruin and all the servants apart from two now dismissed, Mr Rochester instructed John to sell the horses and carriages that so lacked accommodation. Slowly, one piece at a time, horse by horse, carriage by carriage, the wealth and dignity of the Estate was sold off. Well-meaning advisors recommended an auction, but Mr Rochester was unimpressed by the suggestion and showed no interest in it. He could not bear the thought of strangers pawing over those possessions he would once so willingly have made Jane's.

John was offered a general position on the Estate which he declined, preferring to begin a new position as Head Coachman elsewhere. After all, he had received many offers over the years and his name was well-known and well-respected in the great houses of England. Mr Rochester generously paid John his wages and instructed him to take a small covered gig and the horse to pull it. The monies they achieved at the end of John's journey could remain John's.

Loading the obviously pregnant woman everyone would naturally take to be his wife into the gig and collecting what few items they had, at daybreak the next morning John began the long journey to the port of Hull and onto a ship bound for the lucrative trade routes of warm Caribbean seas.

Home and safe at last, Louella introduced John as her husband. Everyone recalled Louella's marriage to 'the English man' and as her husband was undoubtedly English, and still as tall, dark and broodingly handsome as they remembered him, they accepted his identity without question and made him welcome. Louella's half-brother Mason was sworn to secrecy on pain of death if he ever revealed their secret, and as he wasn't the bravest of men, combined with the guilt he felt at Louella's confinement in England, he resigned himself to the situation and resolved to make the best of it. In time he came to value his new brother-in-law even more highly than he had esteemed the first. He soon persuaded himself that fate had indeed dealt Louella a just and fair hand.

• • • •

Although he had prayed for the moment for many years, and although he was relieved that his marriage was finally at an end, when the time came, Mr Rochester couldn't help but feel pity for the woman he had once loved so passionately. Pleased in his own way that his wife's suffering was now at an end, he cared little for the loss of his house. Without his Jane Eyre within its walls, it meant nothing to him.

• • • •

Dear readers, for those of you who are familiar with the story of *Jane Eyre*, you already know the rest.   For those of you who have yet to experience the joys of Charlotte Brontë's original work of *Jane Eyre*, that classical magnum opus of English literature published in 1847, I would invite you to turn to the brief synopsis at the end of this book, or, even better, find and read the original masterpiece.   I hope it brings you as much joy and comfort as it has given me over the years.

Chapter 23

Lisa wondered what she would have done in Louella's place. In the twenty-first century, with equal rights for women, it was easy to think that she would have run away. But to where? What kind of a life would she have lived? Louella had no trade such as sewing skills or knowledge of cooking to support her. It was true that she had a few trinkets left she could have sold to support herself for a short time as the loathsome Grace Poole had not stolen quite all of her memories away. Added to which was the fact that before John had commissioned her boots, apart from her house slippers she didn't even have footwear to flee in, let alone a man to protect her and care for her. As an outsider, who would have believed her story? Besides which, even if they did, as a married woman she was a chattel, and therefore technically her husband's property and responsibility. It was ironic, thought Lisa, that despite the final emancipation and the freeing of all Caribbean slaves in 1838, Louella would still have felt 'owned' as a wife, and just as much a slave, albeit a servant within the lauded state of matrimony.

If Louella had run away, she could have starved by the roadside, or been found and recaptured. She could have been thrown in jail, incarcerated in a mental institution, from which there really would have been no escape. Or perhaps, even worse, found by someone who would have taken advantage of her and sold her on, like a horse, to a house of ill-repute; forced to work for her meagre food rations and lodgings, though her exotic good looks would no doubt have proved popular.

No. Louella had done the right thing to stay where she was within the relative safety and security of the walls of Thornfield Hall; she was better off where she was. On reflection, and given the historical context of the time, Lisa decided that she would have done the same. It was a credit to Louella's strength of character and personality that she hadn't gone mad, but had overcome her isolation and betrayal and the drugs that both Grace Poole and her husband had forced upon her. Besides which, if she had run away, she would never have met John.

Few people in those days had the luxury of marrying for love. For most people marriage was a practical arrangement, decided either by their parents or endorsed by the same, especially amongst the aristocracy and the wealthy. It was hoped that love, or at least some semblance of affectionate companionship, would eventually set seed and grow through the trellis and structure of marriage as a sweet-scented dog rose might seek the sun through the briars of a hedgerow.

Louella had been pregnant when she and John fled England. They had gone on to have three more healthy children. With her own coffee-coloured looks and the startling resemblance to her ancestral grandmother, Lisa's parentage down the female line had could never be in question. She was a part of the great Mason dynasty by blood and fiercely proud of it, despite her heritage being one of the most closely guarded secrets of the West Indies; as precious as the spice routes John and Louella had travelled to finally feel at home, together and free at last.

For Lisa, there were still a number of pieces of the jigsaw puzzle of her life to be discovered and put in place. However, one piece had become much clearer. Having researched the dynamics of relationships and having thought and written so much about them over the previous months, she now had a much better idea of the kind of man she would like to share her life with. Her thoughts and writing had helped her to identify and reveal to herself her ideal partner, although she was very happy to remain flexible about him. The point was, she was happy with herself and her life, she knew what she wanted and, just as importantly, she knew what she didn't want.

She had the strangest kind of feeling that in some way, every day was bringing her ideal future closer ...

Final Word

It was Saturday morning and Lisa was working on the punts in the city centre when she saw a group of young men walking up the street. Well, not young exactly, early thirties rather than mid-twenties, but young enough to still be good-looking and old enough to have become interesting. Stopping on the pavement they looked over the bridge at the punts and then decided to go to one of the coffee bars on the quay so they could watch the comings and goings on the river. They were too well dressed to be students, besides which, Lisa knew that by now she would have seen them around the city, as the Cambridge student population was a relatively small one.

"Oh no, not another crazy stag party up from London. If they're sick in your punt girl, capsize it and cool them all down."

"Words of wisdom, Angela, thanks," laughed Lisa as she rearranged the cushions in her punt and removed the sweet wrappers so kindly left by the last group of excited under-age Italian students. They were here in Cambridge for the summer school their parents hoped would improve their English and subsequent school grades. Lisa thought it a triumph of hope over expectation, as they only ever spoke to each other and that was in Italian.

Lisa had almost forgotten about the group of young men when they emerged from the bar some twenty minutes later. Not for the first time, she noticed one of the men in particular as he approached the punting shed.

"Hi, I'm David, David de Bry. We're here for the weekend. Can you teach us how to drive one of these things?"

137

"Yes, sure, no problem. Up for a stag weekend? Who's getting married?"

"Not me. I'm not that lucky. Maybe one day ..." his voice tailed off

"Well, climb on board. These punts are quite stable if you don't rock the boat too much. Here, give me your hand. I'm Lisa by the way. I'll be your chauffeur for the day."

David made sure that he sat where he could watch Lisa from his vantage point at the end of the boat. He was struck by the easy way she moved her body to control the punt, slightly changing the weight on each of her long slender legs to change direction, leaning into the pole as it rose and sank into the water, moving slowly against the weight of the water so the punt slid along, gliding almost silently across the river's surface.

There was something about her he thought, something about her tight jeans, exposed stomach, long slim arms and lithe dancer's legs. Her tanned skin glowed amber in the afternoon sun and her naked feet, adorned by gold toe rings, caught the sunlight and glinted against the water. The rhythm of the rise and fall of the pole was hypnotic. David felt something stirring. Something deep inside him, although he couldn't quite place where that might be. Looking at Lisa, he didn't think that he had ever seen anyone quite so beautiful.

Author's Epilogue

I wrote this book as a message of hope for anyone who has not yet found a soul mate or a sacred space within their relationship. I wrote it to help you learn about the dynamics of relationships and to heal some of the hurt that your past relationships may have caused you on your journey to where you are now. I wanted, in some way, if I could, to soothe your wounds with the healing balm of insight and some of the understanding that it has taken me half a lifetime to learn. I hope that in some small way my goal has been achieved and that this book will change your life by making a positive contribution to it.

In recreating Louella's and Lisa's futures for you within the pages of this novel, I hope that you will be able to recreate and re-imagine your own future, in ways that make sense and are meaningful to you, so you become a stronger and happier person because of it.

Be kind to yourself. Step out into the world proud and unafraid. Discover those things that you are passionate about, and, if you are not hurting anyone, yourself included, indulge them whenever and wherever you can. Socrates suggested that, *"The unexamined life is not worth living"*. I would suggest that a life without passion is not worth living.

Logan Pearsall Smith, the great American essayist and man of letters, once said, *"What I like in a good author is not what he says, but what he whispers"*. I hope, therefore, that you have enjoyed what I have said, and I hope that you have heard what I have whispered.

A Synopsis of *Jane Eyre*, by Charlotte Brontë, 1847

Jane Eyre is orphaned as a baby. Taken in by a wealthy uncle who adores her she is despised by his wife who, after the death of her husband, eventually sends Jane off to a draconian English boarding school called Lowood. Jane is thoroughly miserable. She has one friend, who dies.

After eight years at the school, Jane comes of age. Now twenty-one and having worked as a teacher at the school for a short time, Jane advertises for a position as governess in a private house and is offered employment at Thornfield Hall in Yorkshire, teaching the French ward of a certain Mr Edward Fairfax Rochester.

Jane is plain and poor, but possessed of honesty, a keen intellect and a strength of character rarely found amongst the society ladies of the age. For the first time in her life, at Thornfield Hall, Jane feels amongst equals, and more than that, she feels valued, respected and strangely at home.

Mr Rochester is a brooding hero. With the hint of a dark past he is pursued by society women whom he finds shallow and insipid and in whom he has no interest. Somewhat inevitably, he and Jane fall in love, although this journey is not without its twists and turns. To be sure of her feelings for him, and to try to force a declaration from her, he tortures Jane emotionally by pretending that he is going to marry the beautiful Blanche Ingram.

Thornfield Hall is not without its mysteries either. Jane hears unexplained laughter from the third floor and the presence of a rather strange servant called Grace Poole unnerves her. One night she finds Mr Rochester asleep in his bed with its curtains aflame.

She saves his life. On another occasion, a mysterious visitor, Richard Mason, is attacked, but we don't know by whom. Jane tends to him but is sworn to secrecy.

After an emotional outburst in the orchard, Jane agrees to marry Mr Rochester. Shortly before the wedding, a grotesque personage enters her bedroom while she is sleeping, tearing her wedding veil in two pieces and trampling it on the floor.

At the church, Mr Rochester is thwarted. At the point when the parson asks if anyone knows of any impediment to the proposed marriage, every bride and groom's worst nightmare comes true and someone steps forward to identify the existence of Mr Rochester's first wife. According to Charlotte Brontë, it transpires that Mr Rochester's first wife is mad and has been locked up by him on the third floor of Thornfield Hall for the past ten years. Jane is shocked and distraught that her dreams for such a complete and happy union should be thus ruined, and she flees the house.

Mr Rochester is devastated. He is mad with grief. He searches throughout England for Jane, but fails to find her.

Jane escapes on foot with what little money she has and takes a stagecoach to she knows not where. When her money runs out, the stagecoach leaves her on the desolate moors where she lays down to die. She is found by the local Minister, St. John Rivers, who picks her up in his arms and carries her across the moor to his own home where his two sisters care for her. Once Jane recovers she becomes the local school teacher for a year. St. John asks Jane to marry him and go abroad to be a missionary. She does not love him, nor he her. Not able to forget Mr Rochester, Jane refuses to live without passion and turns St. John down.

141

Another uncle dies and leaves Jane a wealthy woman. She shares the money equally with St. John and his two sisters, who neatly turn out to be her long-lost cousins. No longer poor, she resolves to return to Thornfield and discover what has happened to Mr Rochester, and to stay with him as his companion, even if he is still technically married.

Upon her arrival at Thornfield Hall, Jane finds it an empty, burned out shell. The first Mrs Rochester had set fire to the place some time before. She died after jumping from the roof. Mr Rochester tried to save her but failed. A beam fell on him. His once ruggedly handsome face now scarred, he is not only blind, but crippled by the remains of a useless hand.

Now that her hero is a free man, Jane offers up one of the most famous lines in English literary history: *"Reader, I married him"*. Jane Eyre and Mr Rochester, finally equals in spirit, passion and almost in wealth, live happily ever after and go on to have at least two children. Jane's hero regains some sight in one eye and all is as it should be, with love finally triumphant.